WITHDRAWN

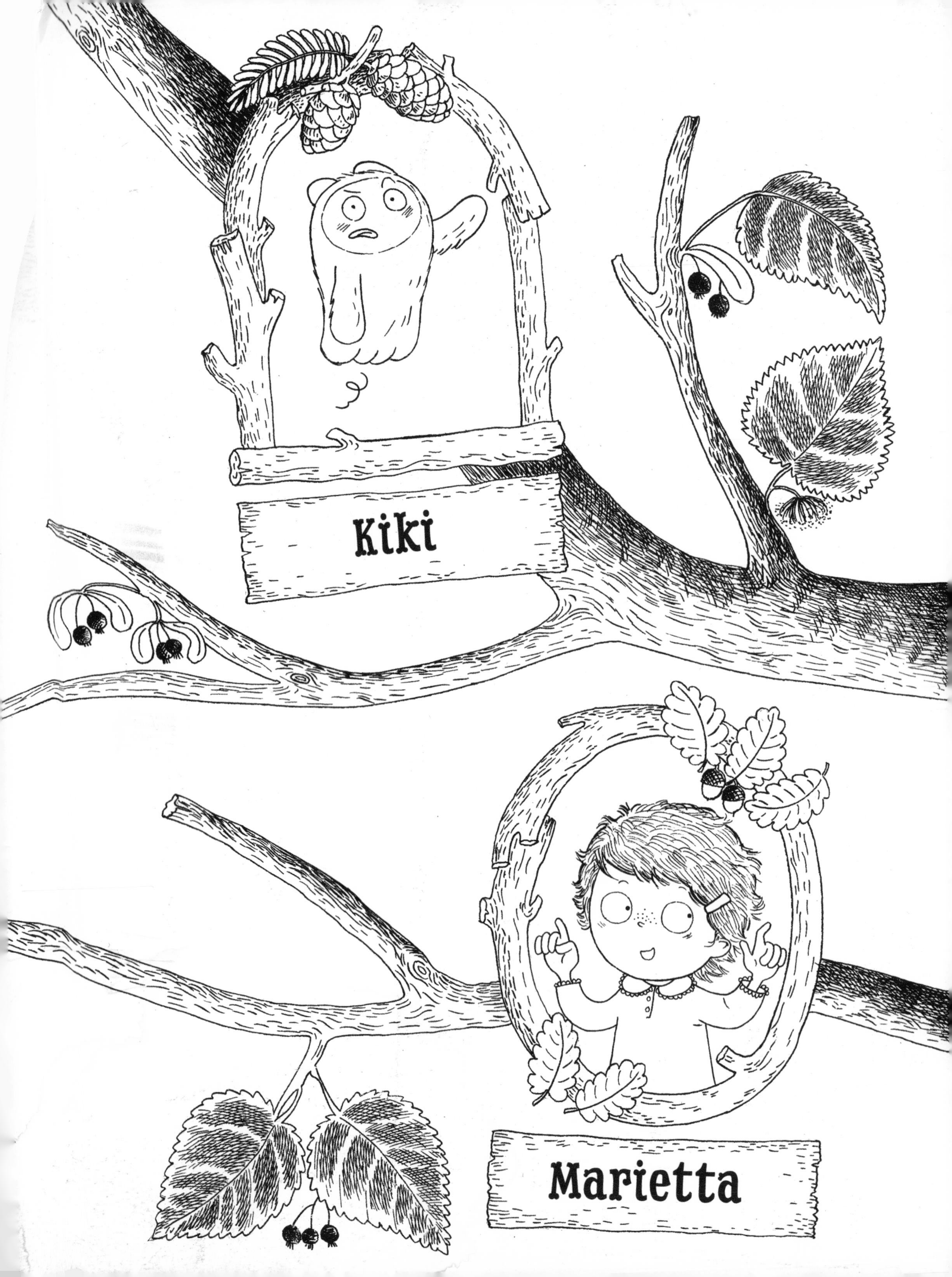
Kiki
Marietta

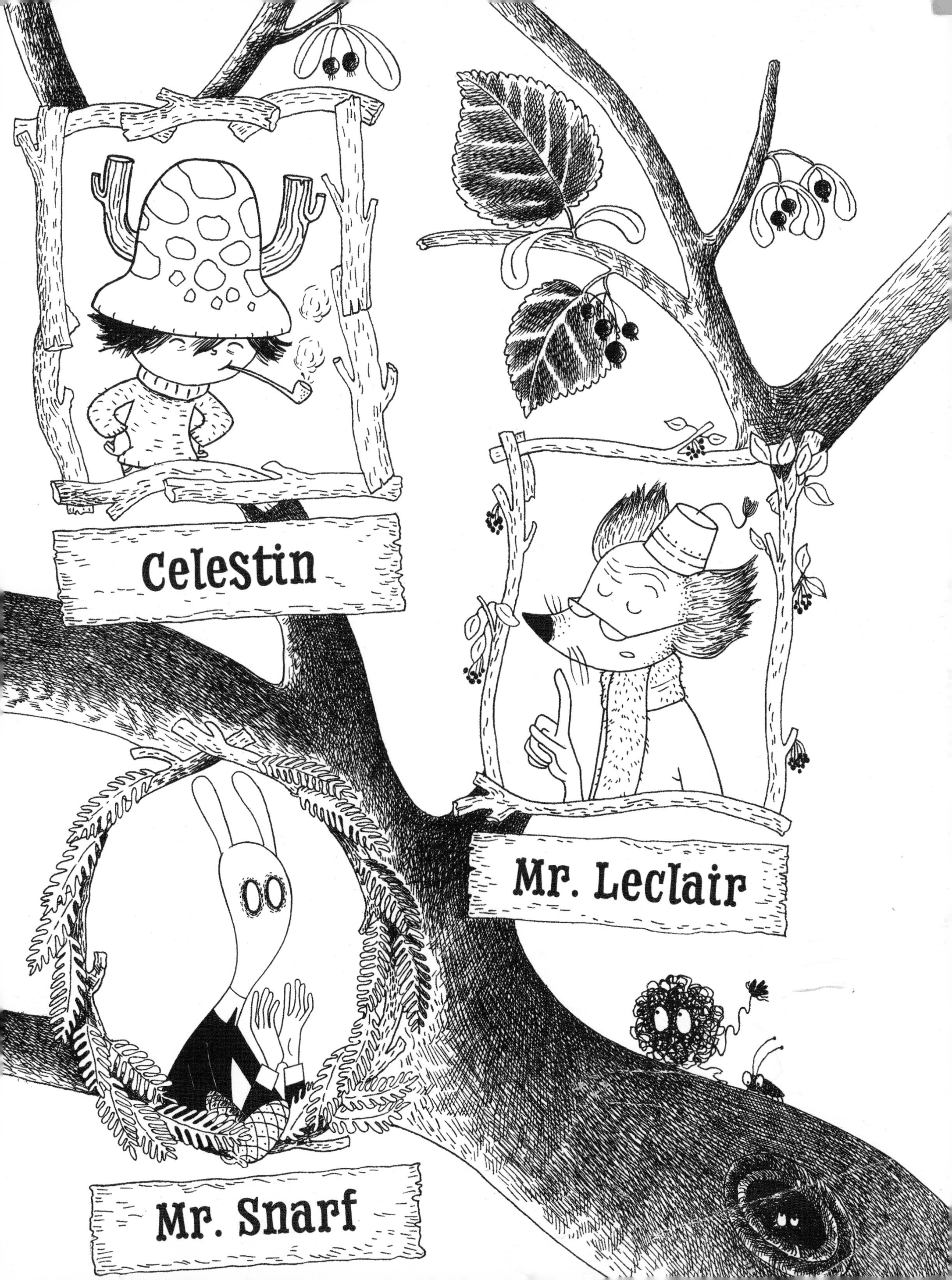
Celestin
Mr. Leclair
Mr. Snarf

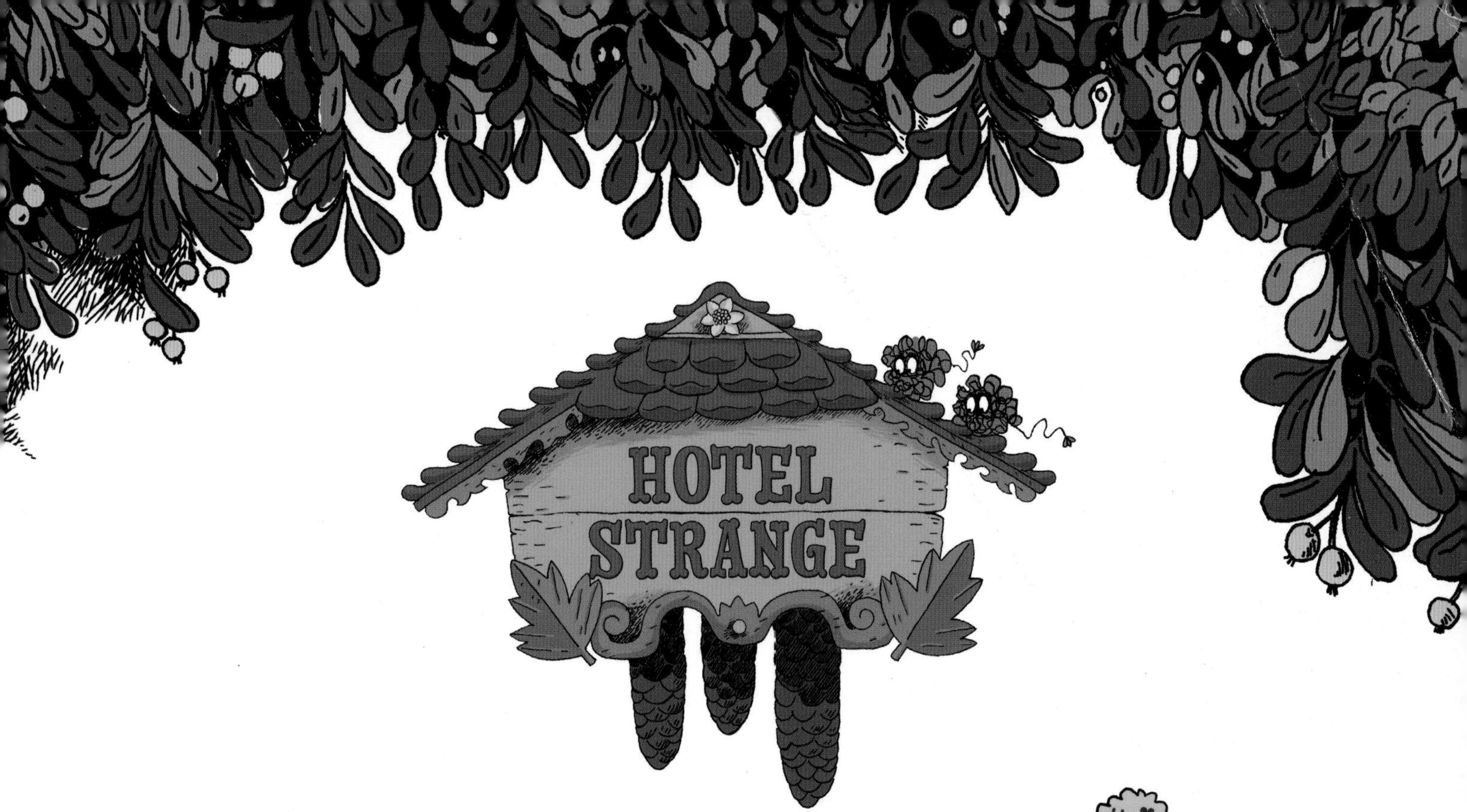
HOTEL
STRANGE

The Ghosts in the Clouds #4

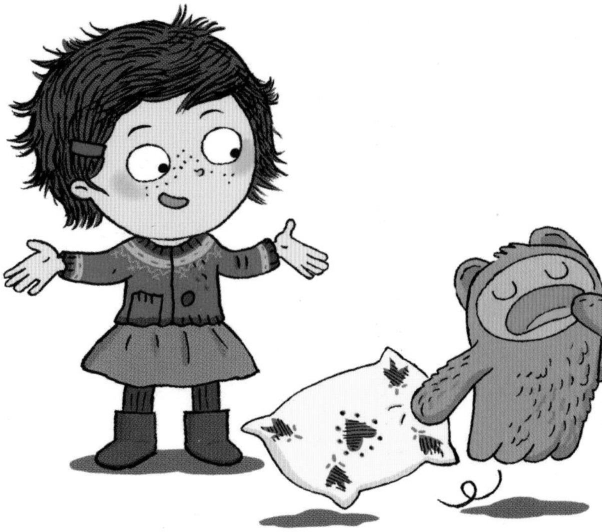

Florian and Katherine Ferrier
illustrations and coloring by Katherine Ferrier

Graphic Universe™ • Minneapolis

Story by Florian and Katherine Ferrier
Illustrations and coloring by Katherine Ferrier
Translation by Carol Klio Burrell

First American edition published in 2017 by Graphic Universe™

Graphic Universe™
A division of Lerner Publishing Group, Inc.
241 First Avenue North
Minneapolis, MN 55401 USA

For reading levels and more information, look up this title at www.lernerbooks.com.

Main body text set in Andy Std 12.5/13.5. Typeface provided by Monotype.

Library of Congress Cataloging-in-Publication Data

Names: Ferrier, Florian. | Ferrier, Katherine, author, illustrator. | Burrell, Carol Klio, translator.
Title: The ghosts in the clouds / Florian and Katherine Ferrier ; illustrations and coloring by Katherine Ferrier ; translation by Carol Klio Burrell.
Other titles: Des fantomes dans les nuages. English
Description: First American edition. | Minneapolis : Graphic Universe, 2016.| Series: Hotel Strange ; #4 | Originally published in Paris by Éditions Sarbacane in 2013 under title: Des fantómes dans les nuages. | Summary: When a group of ghosts takes Mr. Snarf away, the other animal residents of Hotel Strange fly into the clouds, hoping to retrieve their friend.
Identifiers: LCCN 2016009477 (print) | LCCN 2016029307 (ebook) | ISBN 9781467785877 (lb : alk. paper) | ISBN 9781512427042 (eb pdf)
Subjects: LCSH: Graphic novels. | CYAC: Graphic novels. | Hotels, motels, etc.—Fiction. | Ghosts—Fiction. | Animals—Fiction.
Classification: LCC PZ7.7.F48 Gh 2016 (print) | LCC PZ7.7.F48 (ebook) | DDC 741.5/973—dc23

LC record available at https://lccn.loc.gov/2016009477

Manufactured in the United States of America
1-37940-19398-3/8/2016

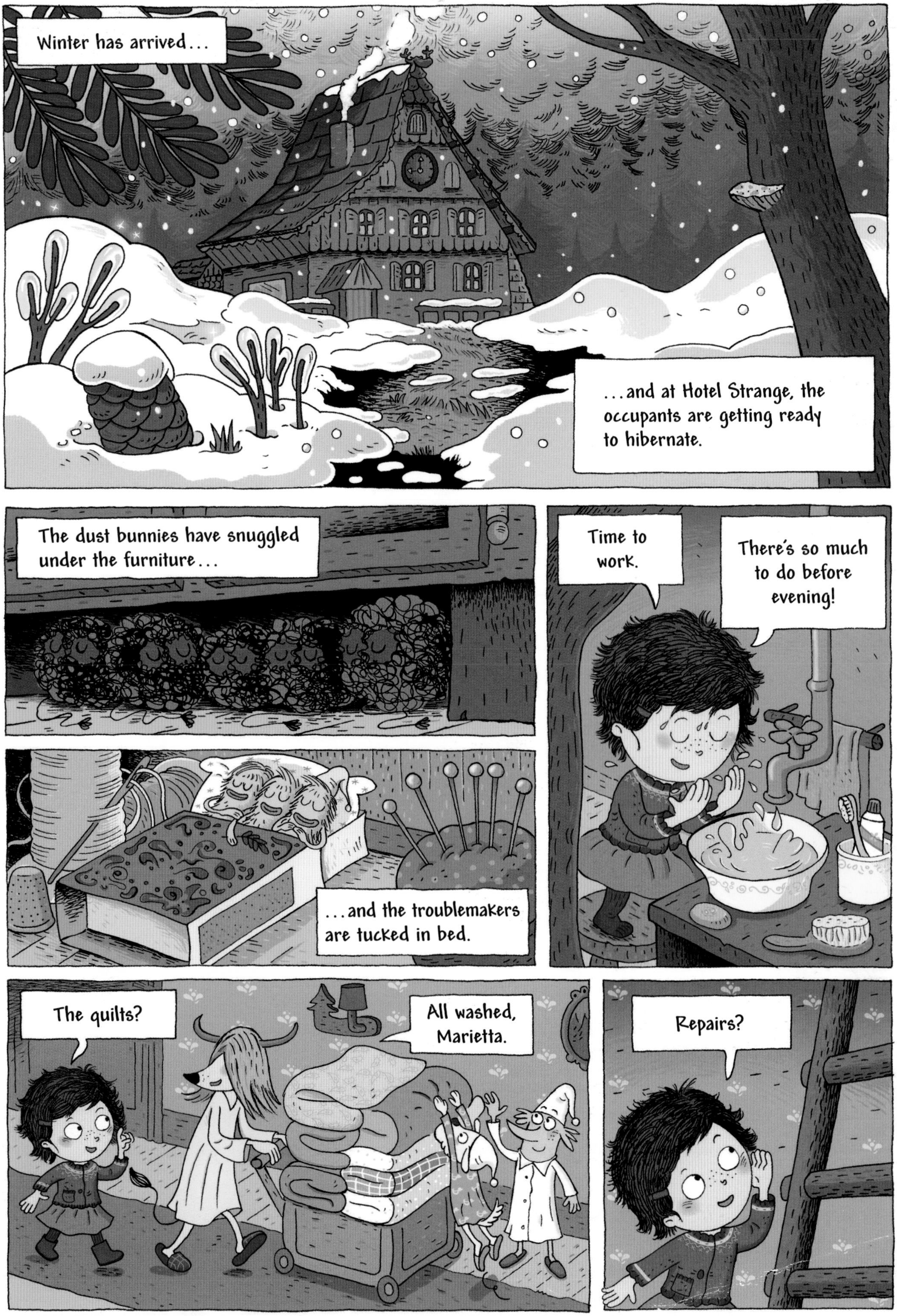

Winter has arrived...
...and at Hotel Strange, the occupants are getting ready to hibernate.
The dust bunnies have snuggled under the furniture...
...and the troublemakers are tucked in bed.
Time to work.
There's so much to do before evening!
The quilts?
All washed, Marietta.
Repairs?

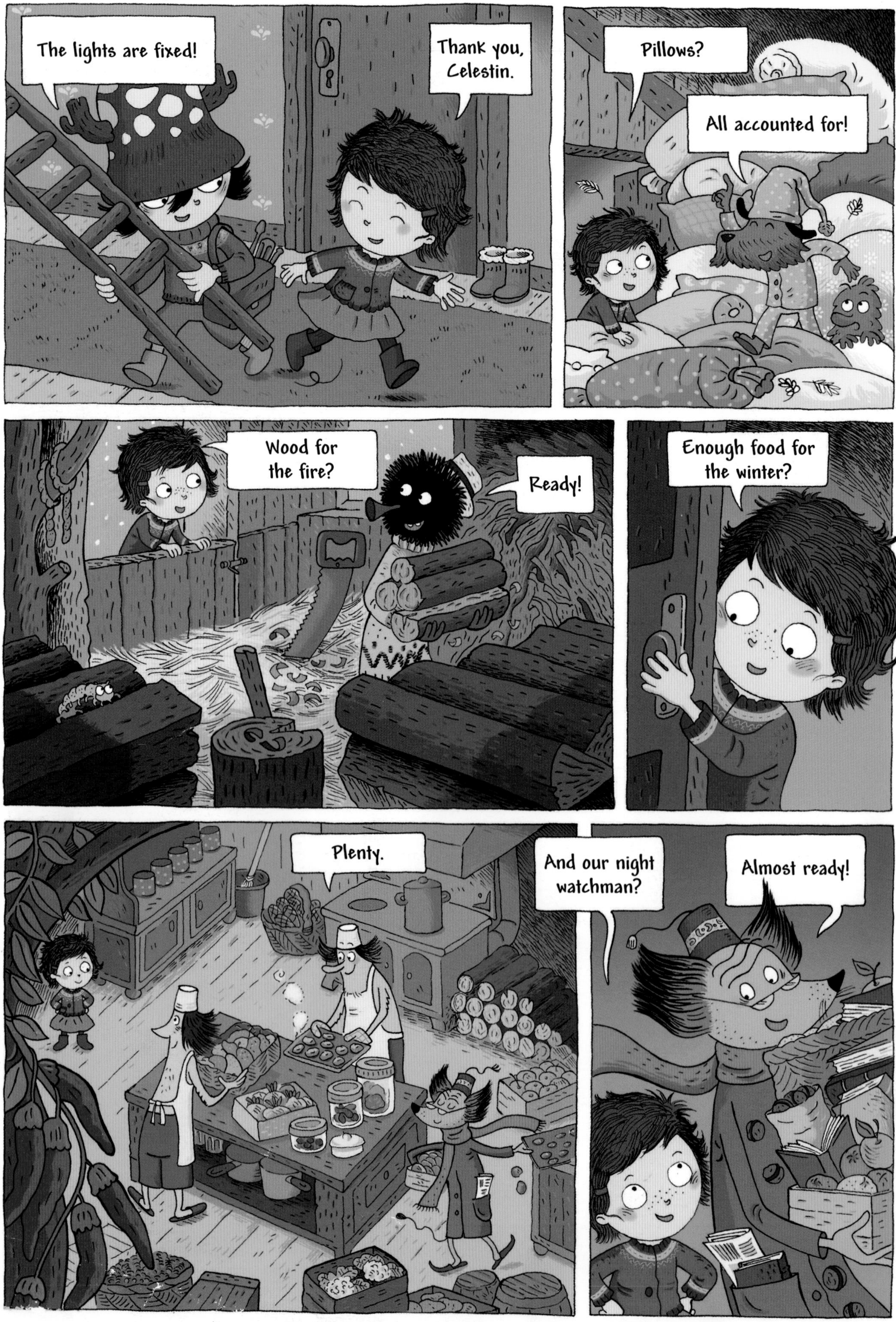
The lights are fixed!
Thank you, Celestin.
Pillows?
All accounted for!
Wood for the fire?
Ready!
Enough food for the winter?
Plenty.
And our night watchman?
Almost ready!

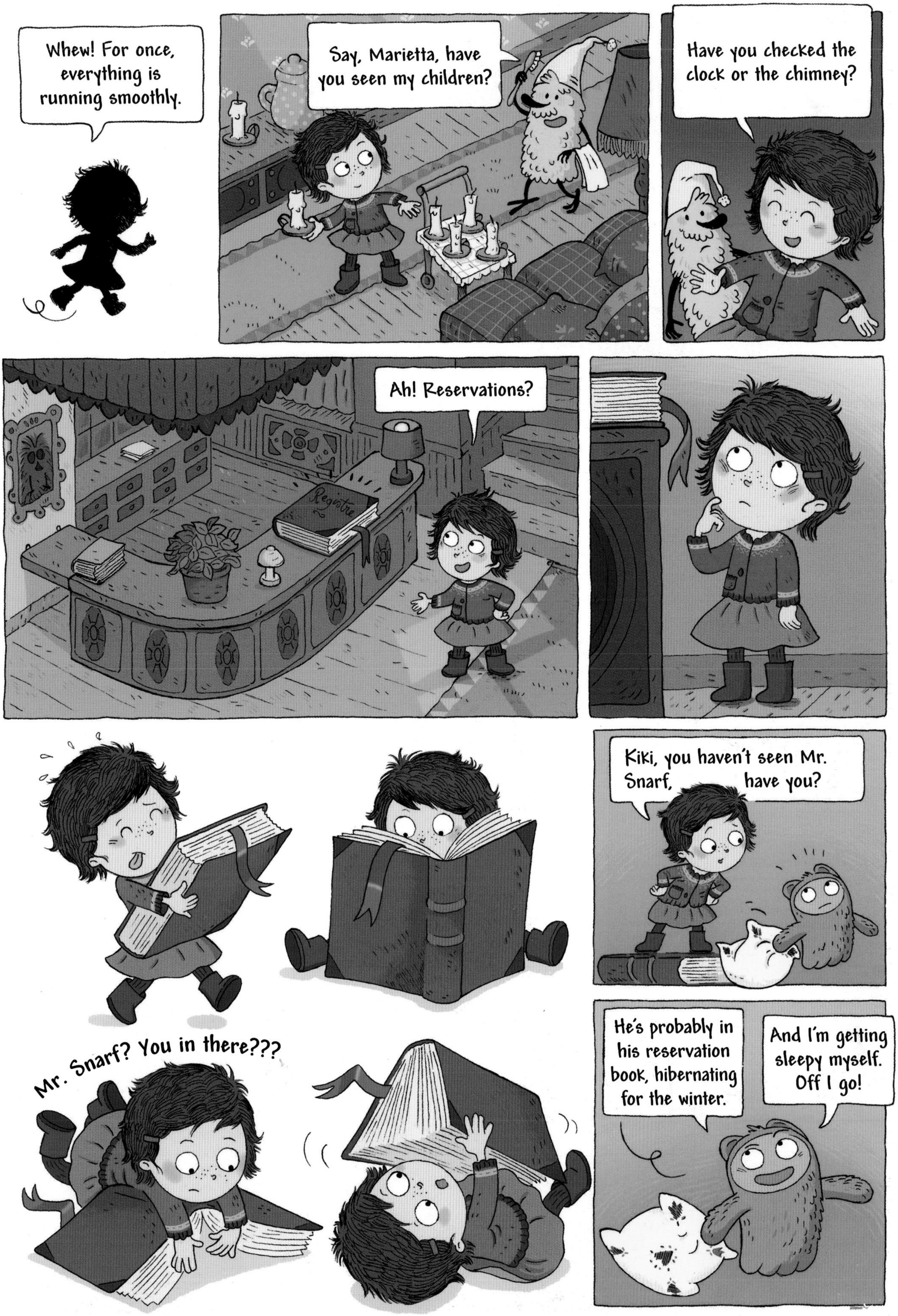
Whew! For once, everything is running smoothly.
Say, Marietta, have you seen my children?
Have you checked the clock or the chimney?
Ah! Reservations?
Registre
Kiki, you haven't seen Mr. Snarf, have you?
Mr. Snarf? You in there???
He's probably in his reservation book, hibernating for the winter.
And I'm getting sleepy myself. Off I go!

Mr. Leclair, have you seen my children?

AAAAAAH!

Mr. Snarf is all frozen!

Snarf! Say something!

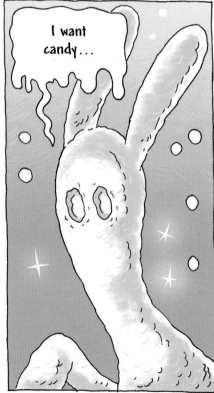

I want candy...

...lots of candy.

6

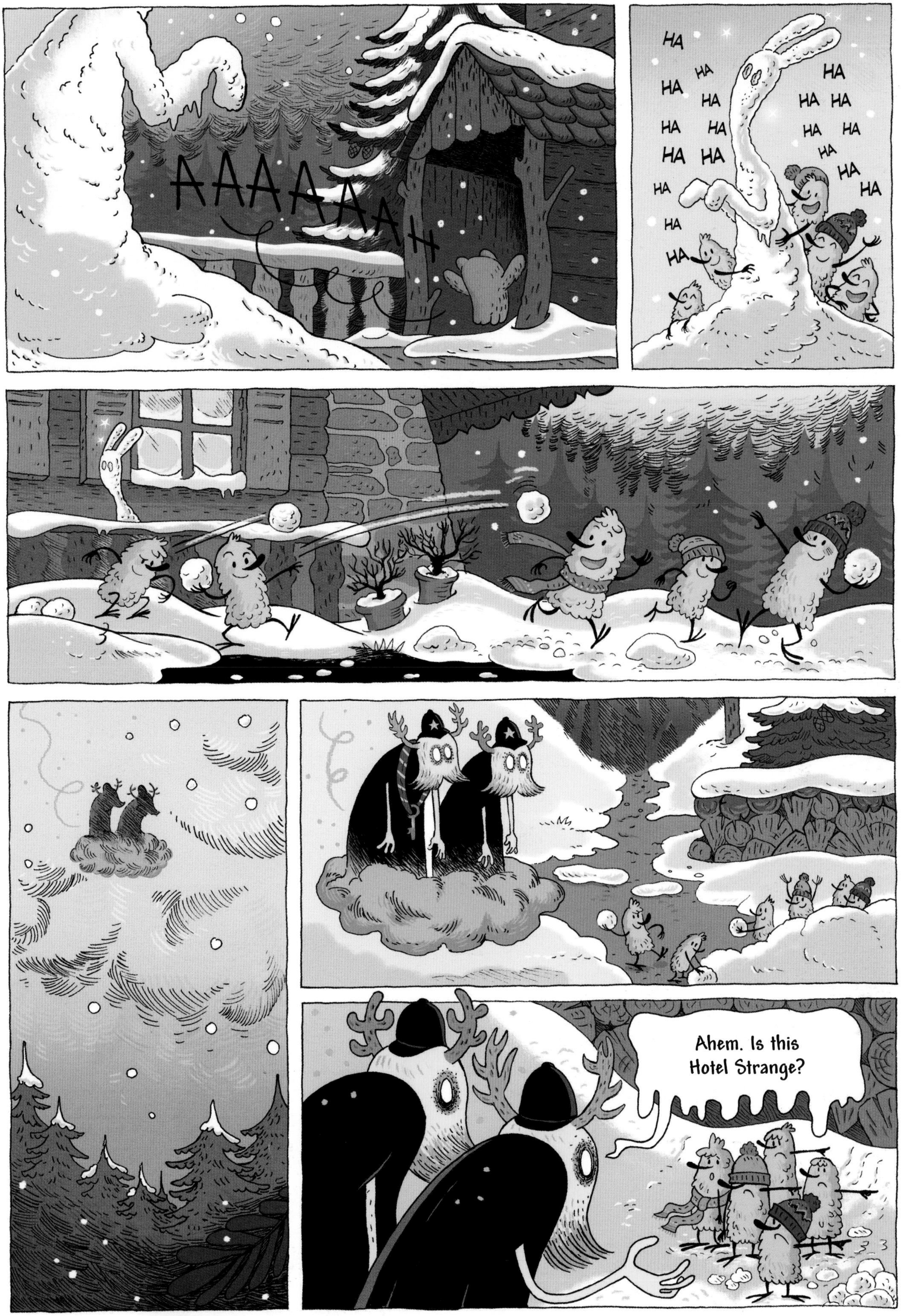
AAAAAAAH
HA HA HA HA HA HA HA HA HA HA HA HA HA HA HA HA HA HA HA HA
Ahem. Is this Hotel Strange?

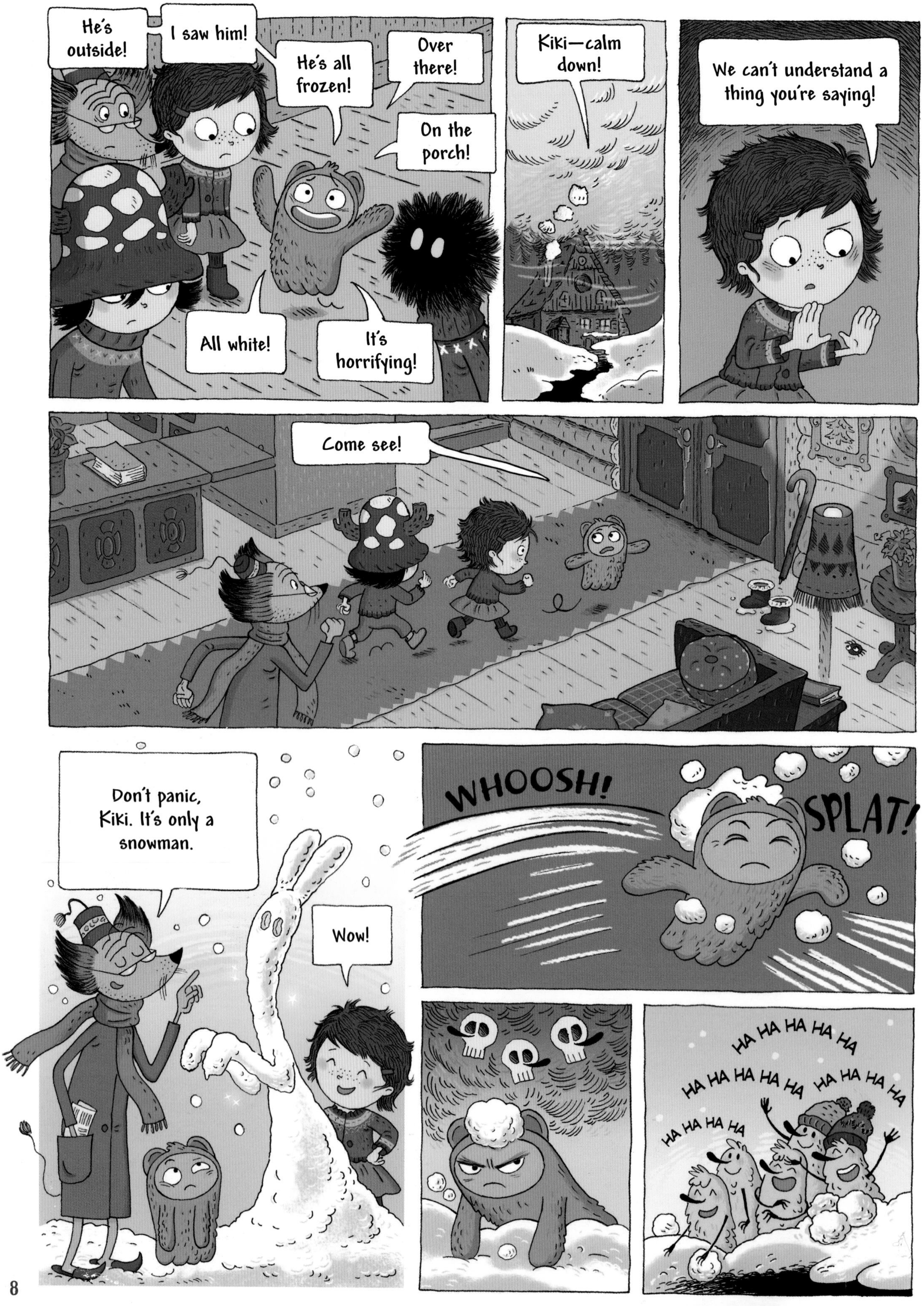
He's outside!
I saw him!
He's all frozen!
Over there!
On the porch!
All white!
It's horrifying!
Kiki—calm down!
We can't understand a thing you're saying!
Come see!
Don't panic, Kiki. It's only a snowman.
Wow!
WHOOSH!
SPLAT!
HA HA HA HA HA
HA HA HA HA HA
HA HA HA HA
HA HA HA HA

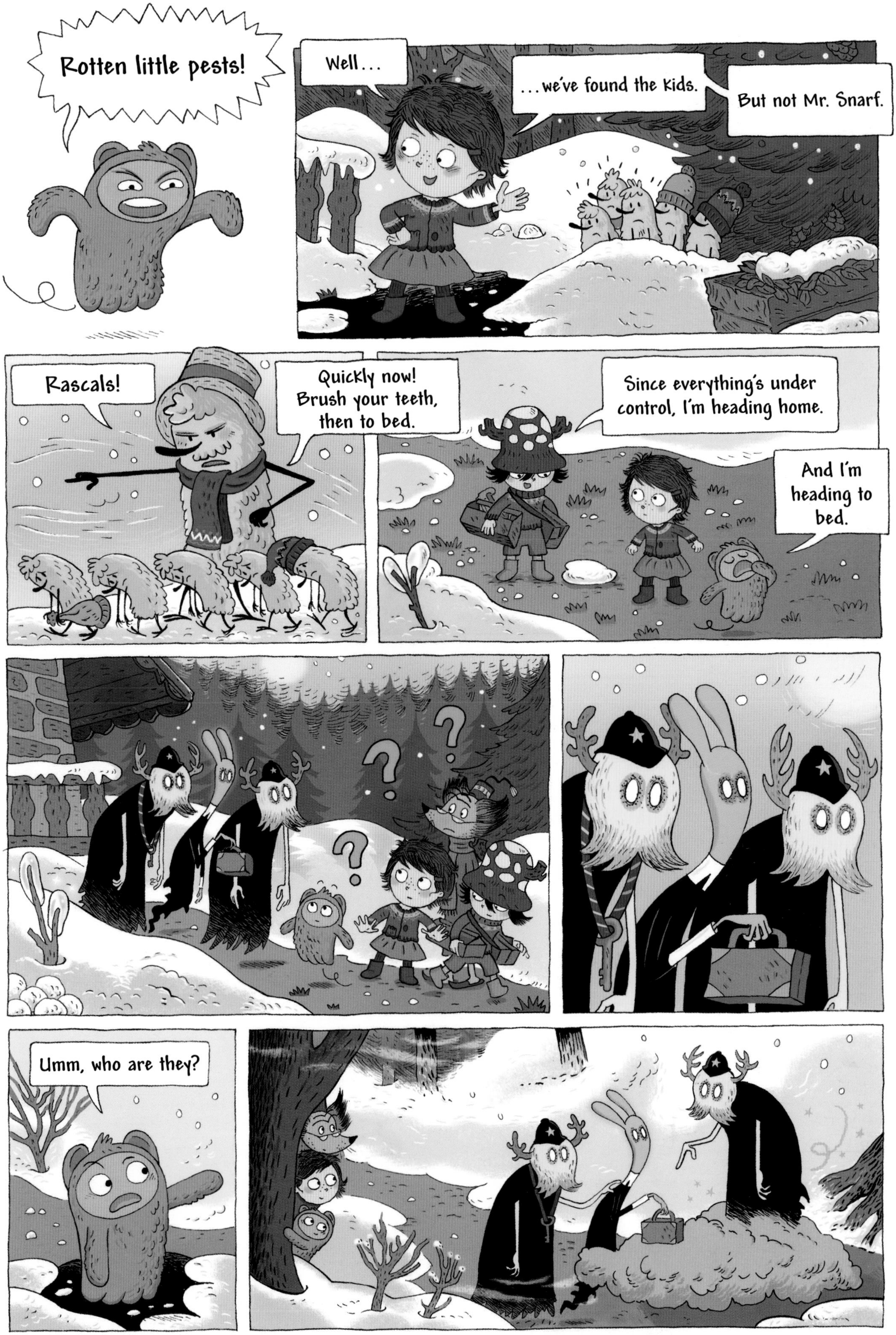

Rotten little pests!
Well...
...we've found the kids.
But not Mr. Snarf.
Rascals!
Quickly now! Brush your teeth, then to bed.
Since everything's under control, I'm heading home.
And I'm heading to bed.
Umm, who are they?

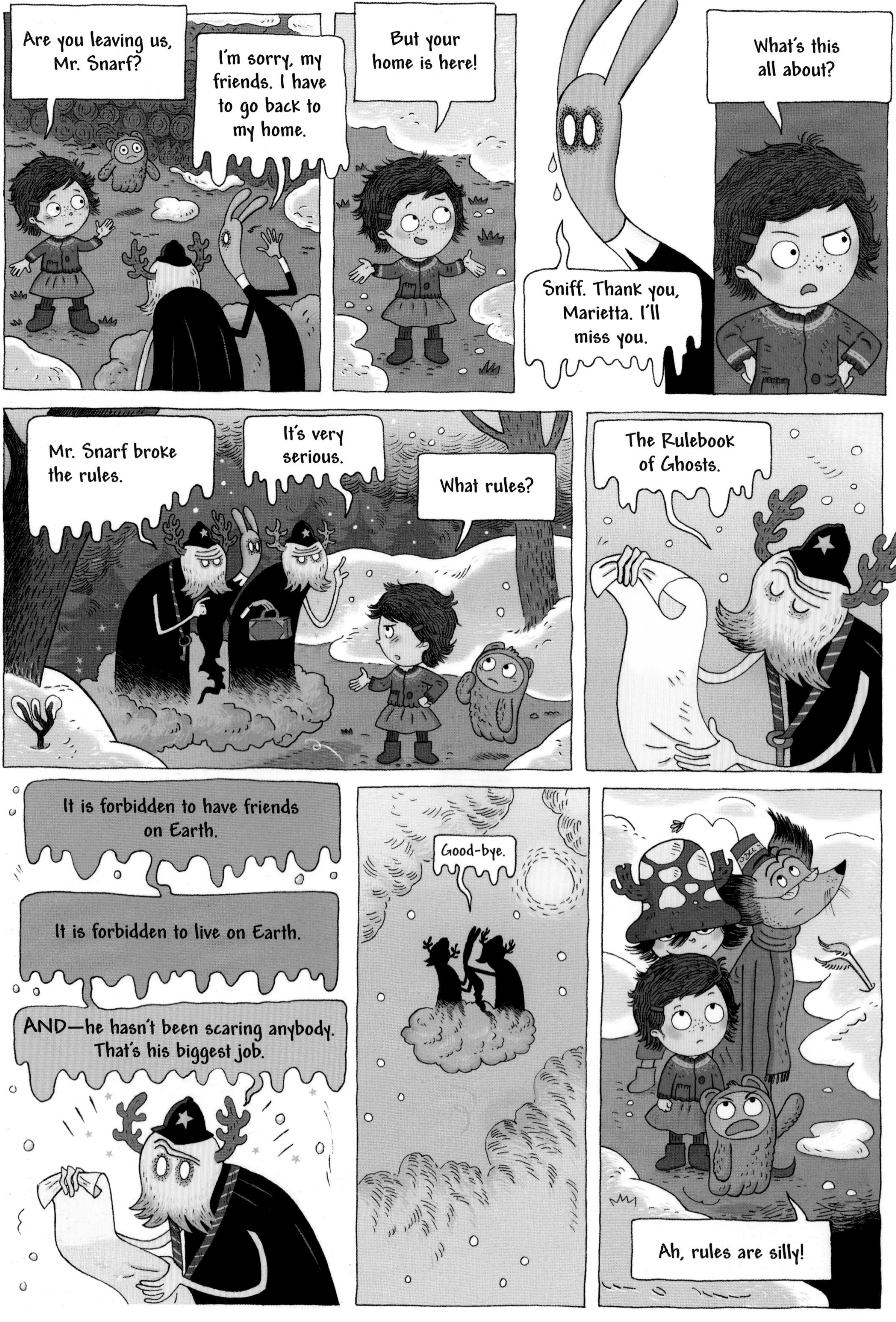

Are you leaving us, Mr. Snarf?
I'm sorry, my friends. I have to go back to my home.
But your home is here!
Sniff. Thank you, Marietta. I'll miss you.
What's this all about?
Mr. Snarf broke the rules.
It's very serious.
What rules?
The Rulebook of Ghosts.
It is forbidden to have friends on Earth.
It is forbidden to live on Earth.
AND—he hasn't been scaring anybody. That's his biggest job.
Good-bye.
Ah, rules are silly!

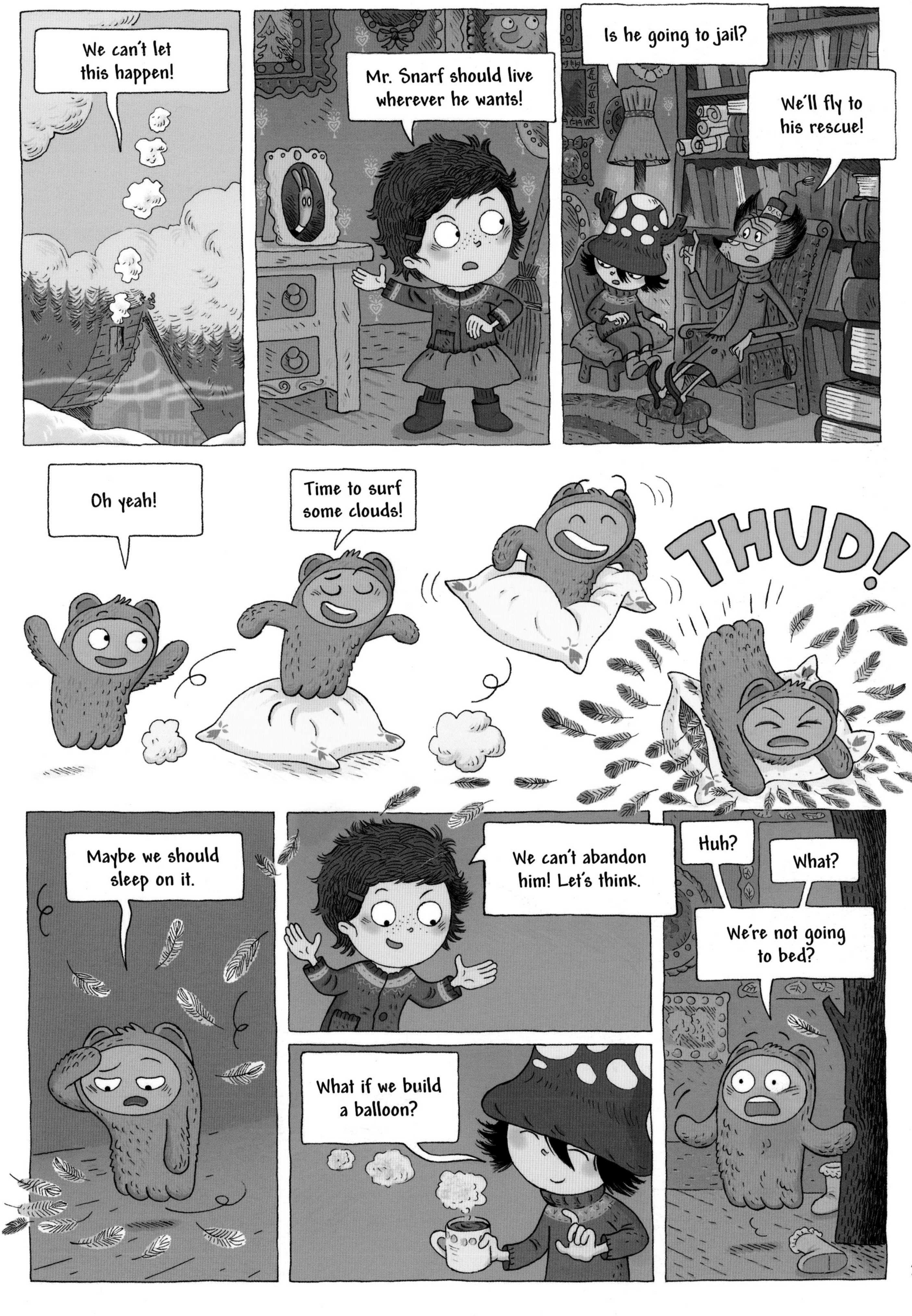
We can't let this happen!
Mr. Snarf should live wherever he wants!
Is he going to jail?
We'll fly to his rescue!
Oh yeah!
Time to surf some clouds!
THUD!
Maybe we should sleep on it.
We can't abandon him! Let's think.
What if we build a balloon?
Huh?
What?
We're not going to bed?

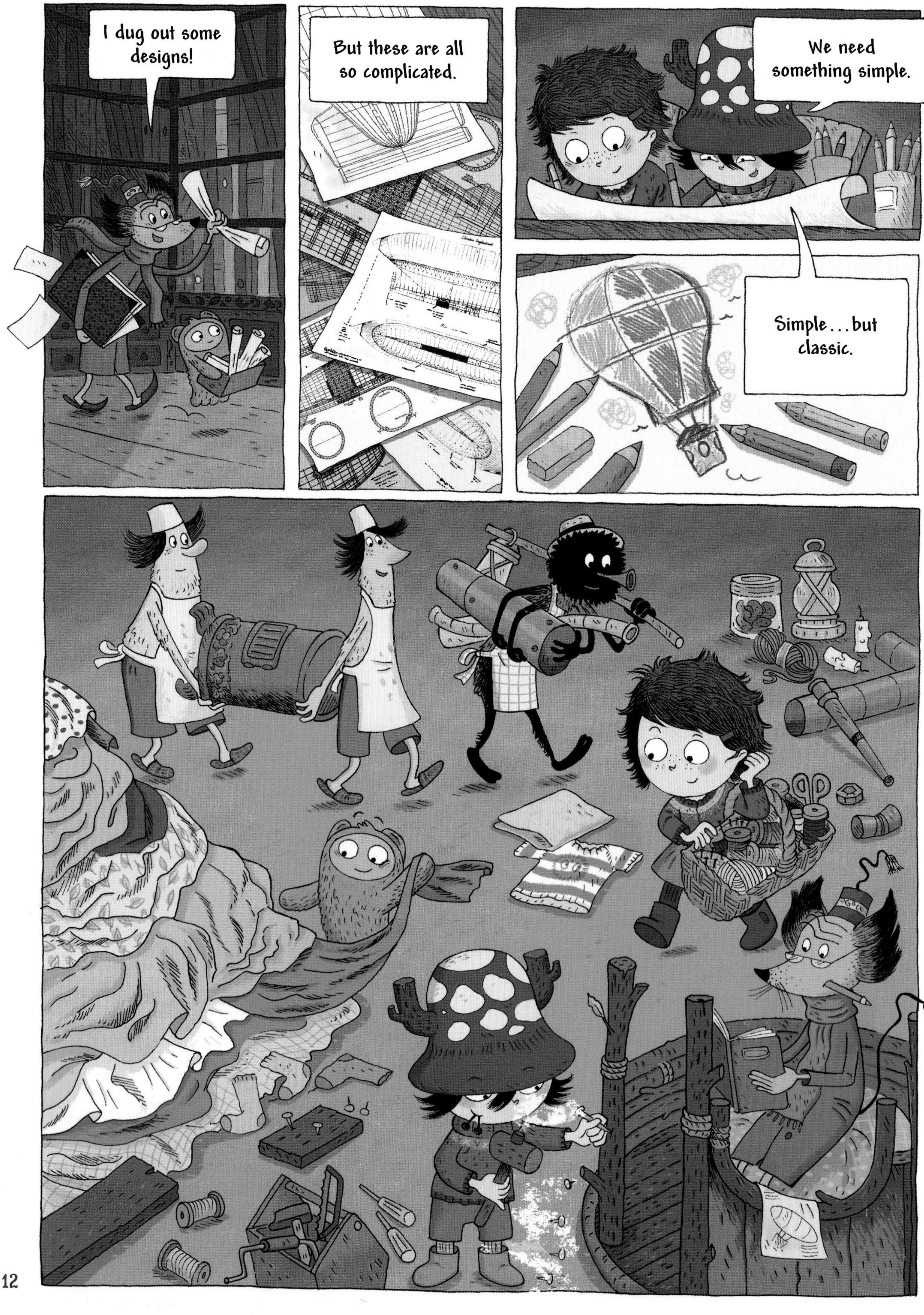
I dug out some designs!
But these are all so complicated.
We need something simple.
Simple...but classic.

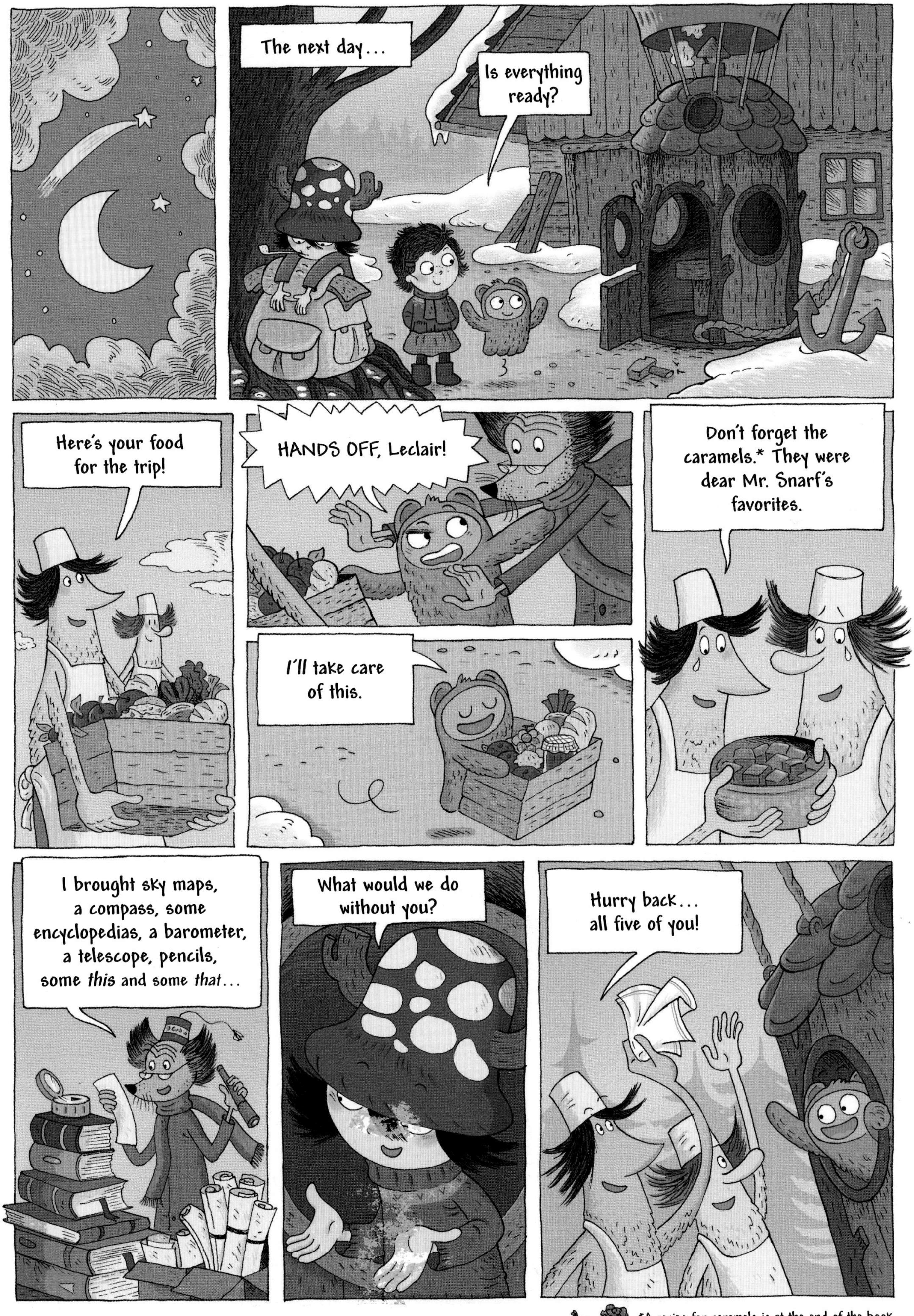
The next day...
Is everything ready?
Here's your food for the trip!
HANDS OFF, Leclair!
I'll take care of this.
Don't forget the caramels.* They were dear Mr. Snarf's favorites.
I brought sky maps, a compass, some encyclopedias, a barometer, a telescope, pencils, some *this* and some *that*...
What would we do without you?
Hurry back... all five of you!

*A recipe for caramels is at the end of the book.

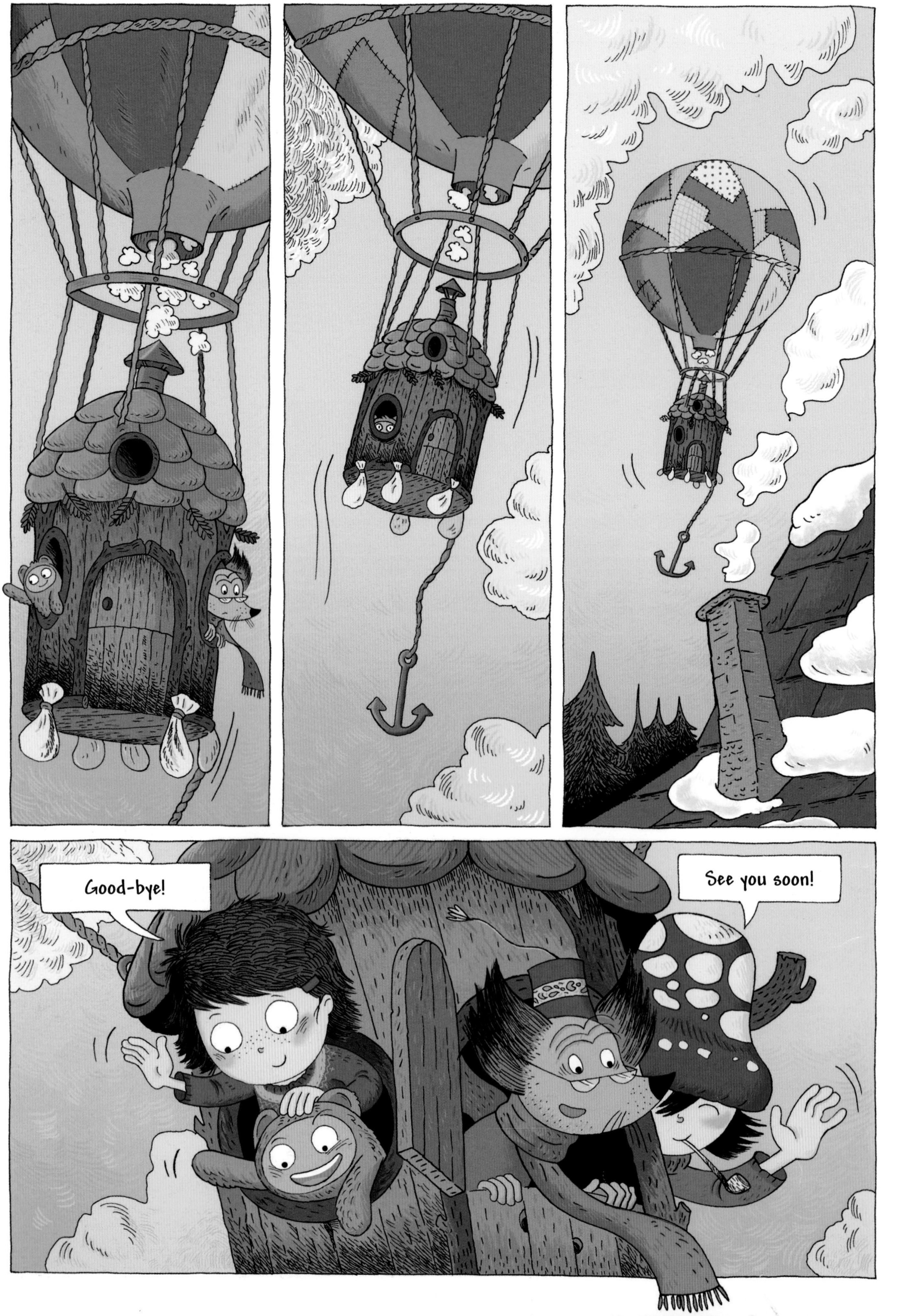
Good-bye!
See you soon!

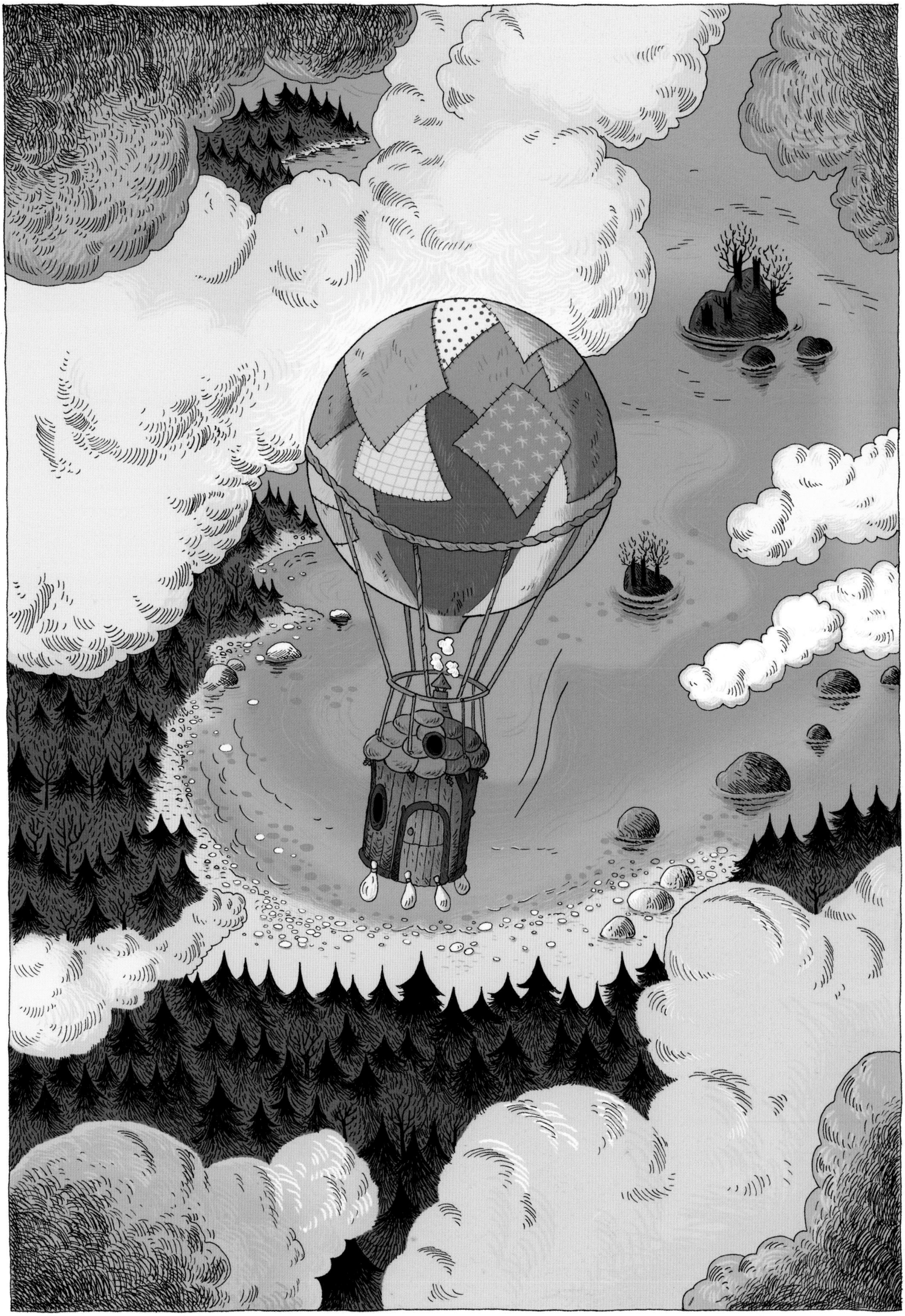

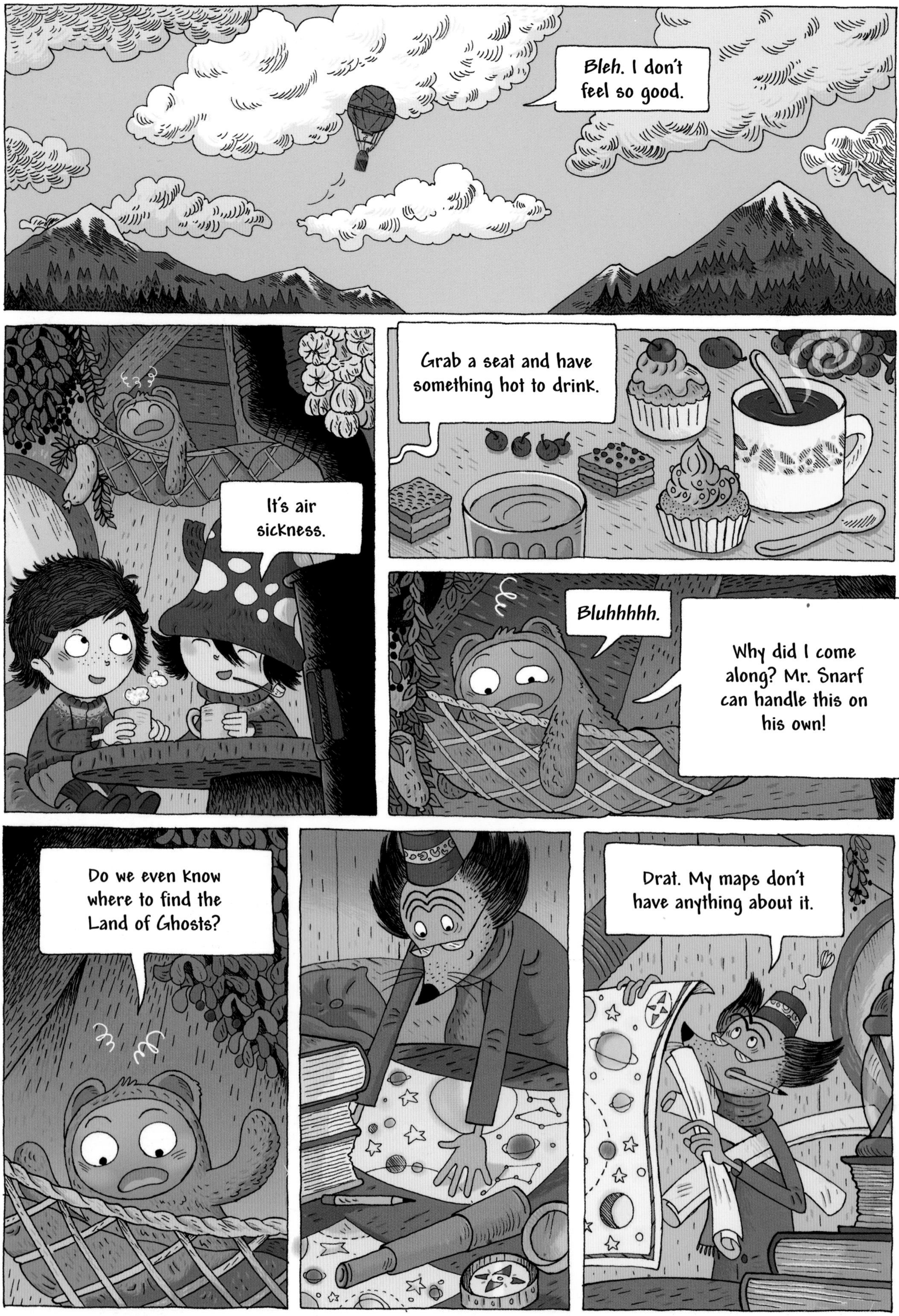
Bleh. I don't feel so good.
Grab a seat and have something hot to drink.
It's air sickness.
Bluhhhhh.
Why did I come along? Mr. Snarf can handle this on his own!
Do we even know where to find the Land of Ghosts?
Drat. My maps don't have anything about it.

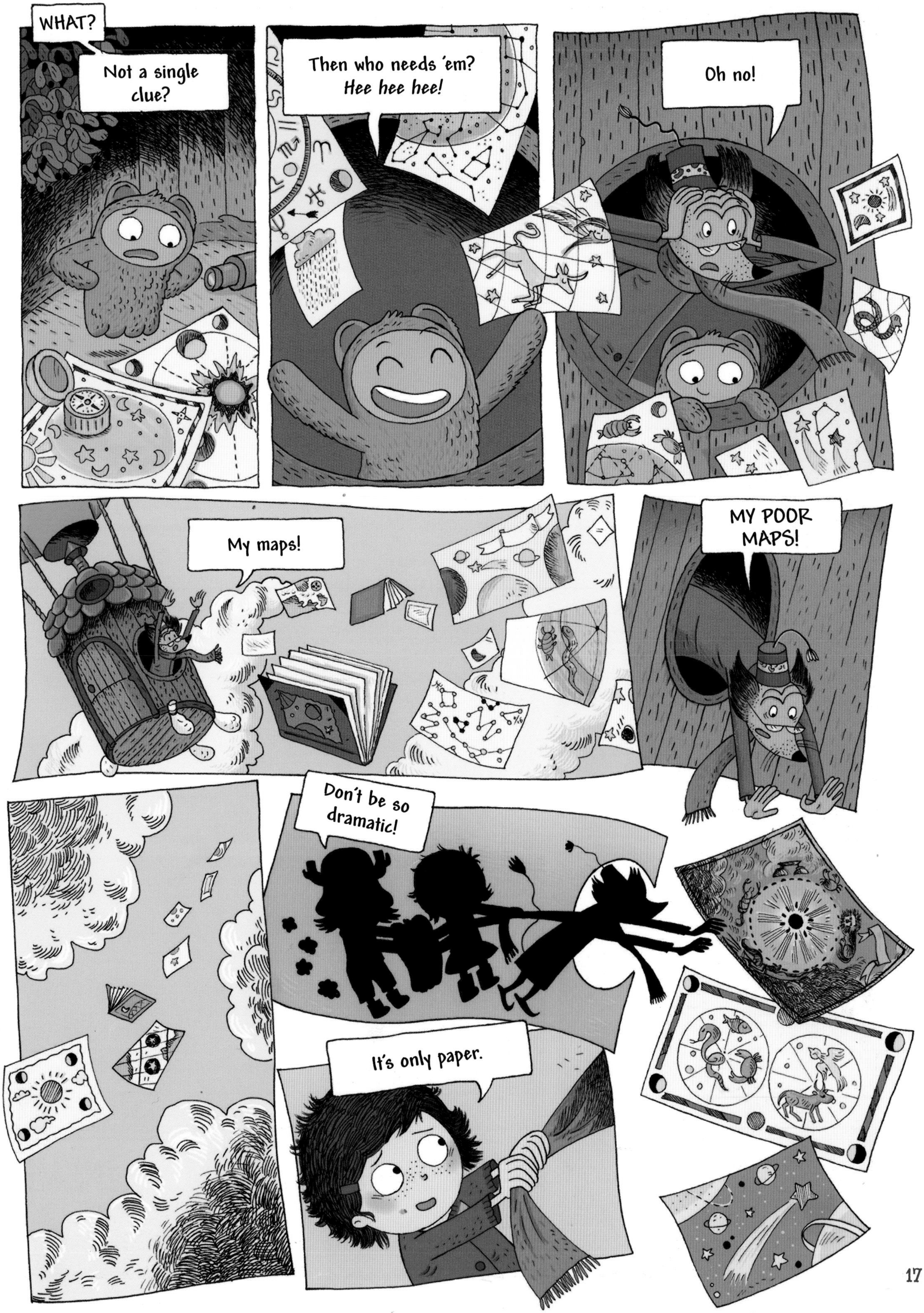
WHAT?
Not a single clue?
Then who needs 'em? *Hee hee hee!*
Oh no!
My maps!
MY POOR MAPS!
Don't be so dramatic!
It's only paper.

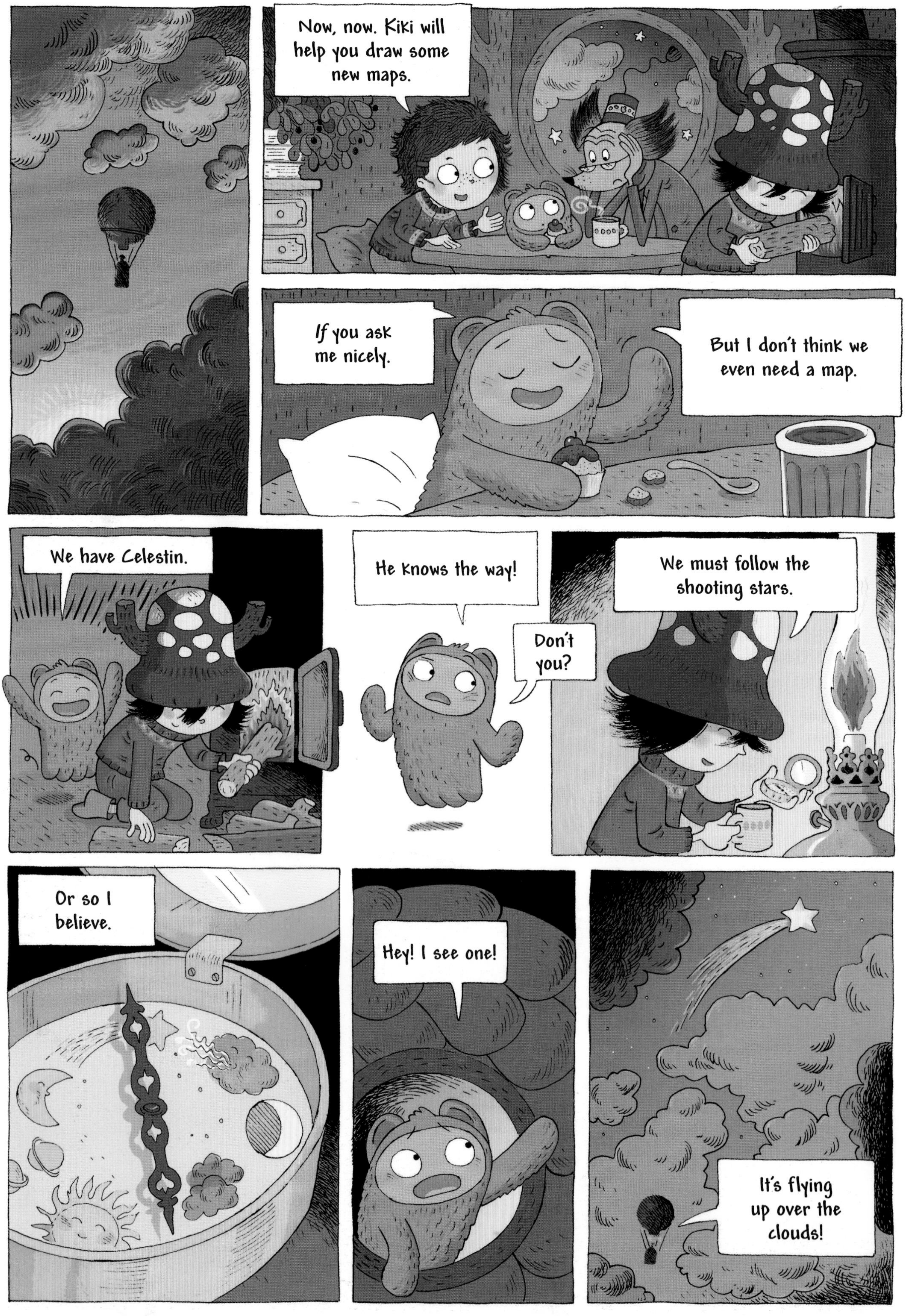
Now, now. Kiki will help you draw some new maps.
If you ask me nicely.
But I don't think we even need a map.
We have Celestin.
He knows the way!
Don't you?
We must follow the shooting stars.
Or so I believe.
Hey! I see one!
It's flying up over the clouds!

We can't catch it! We're too heavy.

It's no use!

Tornado!

Tornaaaado!

Tornaaado!

Tornaado!

Oh no! The weather's turning bad!

AAAAAA

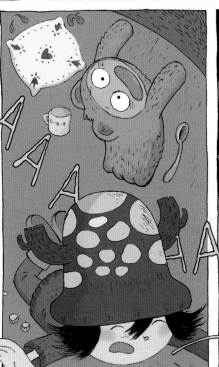

AAA

HAHH!

19

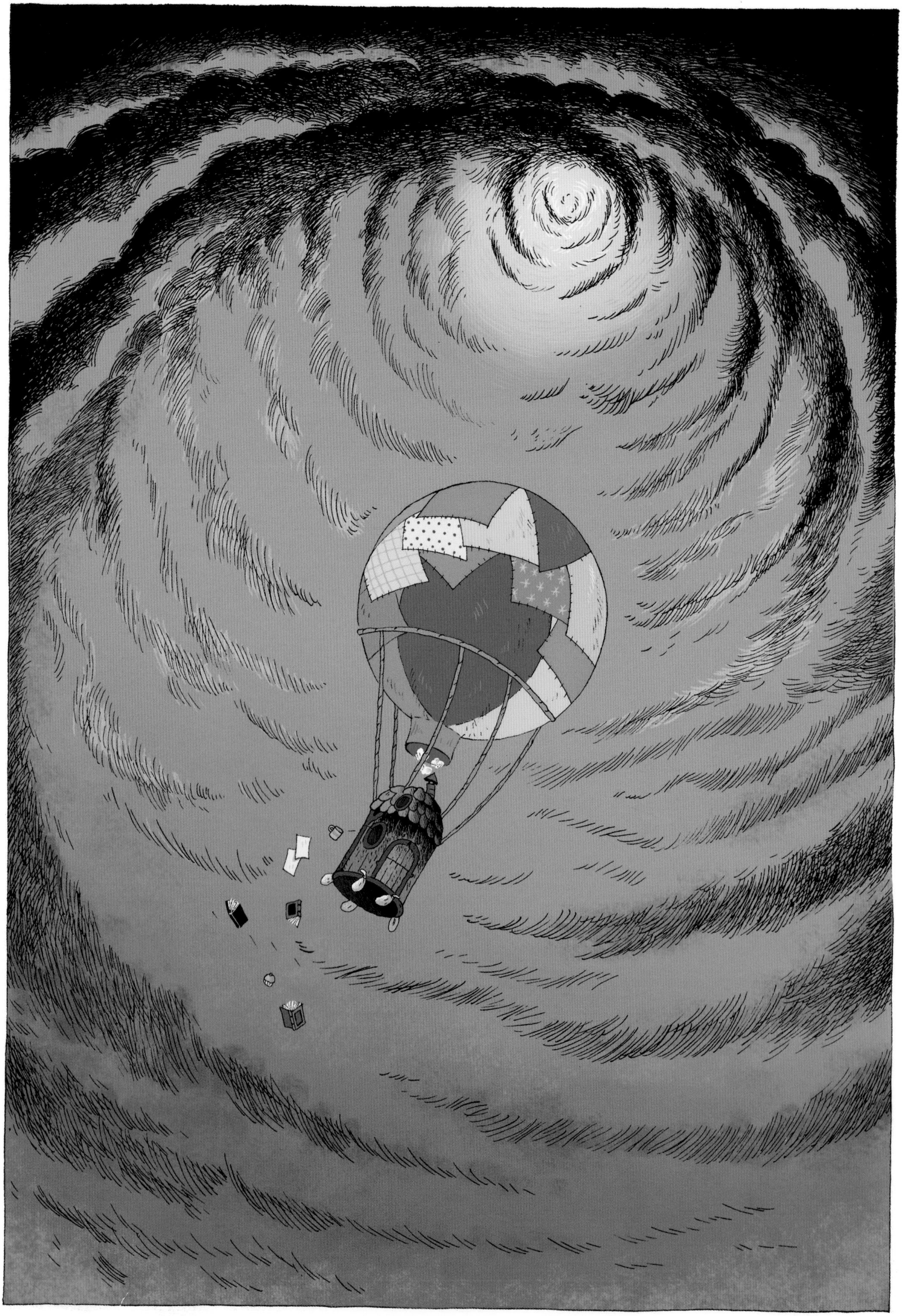

It's spiiiiiinniiing...
I should have stayed home...
There!

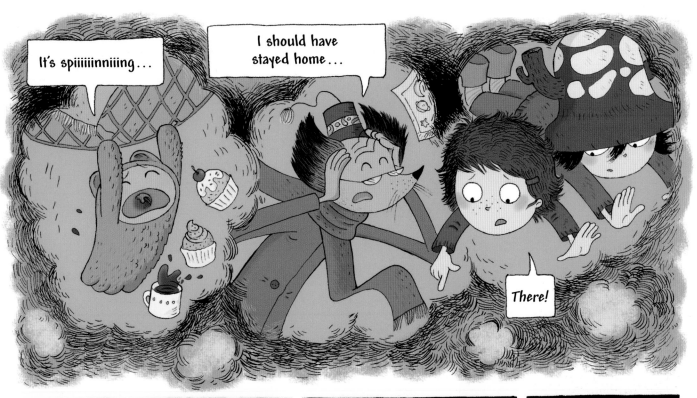

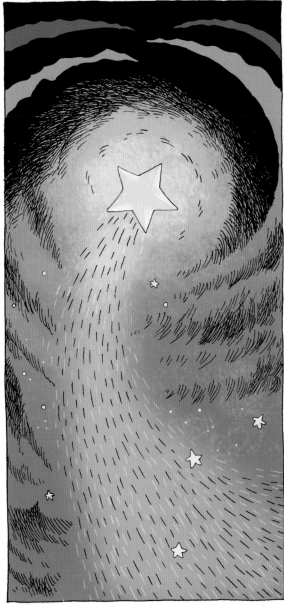

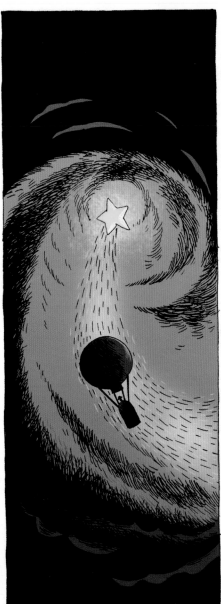

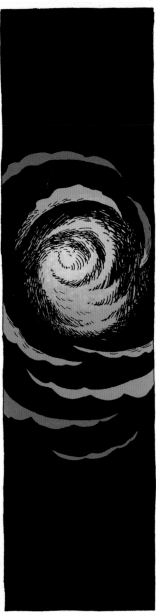

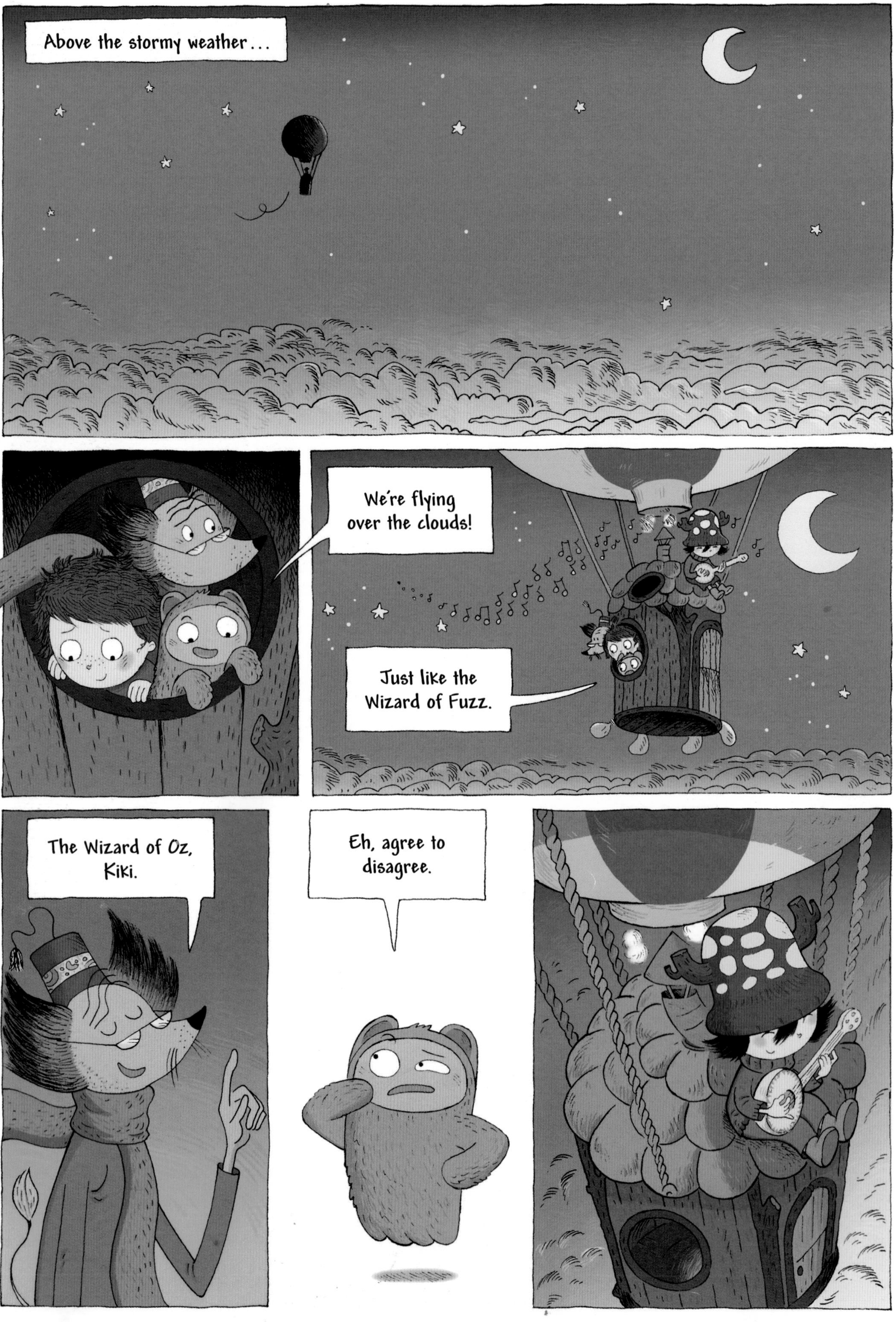

Above the stormy weather...
We're flying over the clouds!
Just like the Wizard of Fuzz.
The Wizard of Oz, Kiki.
Eh, agree to disagree.

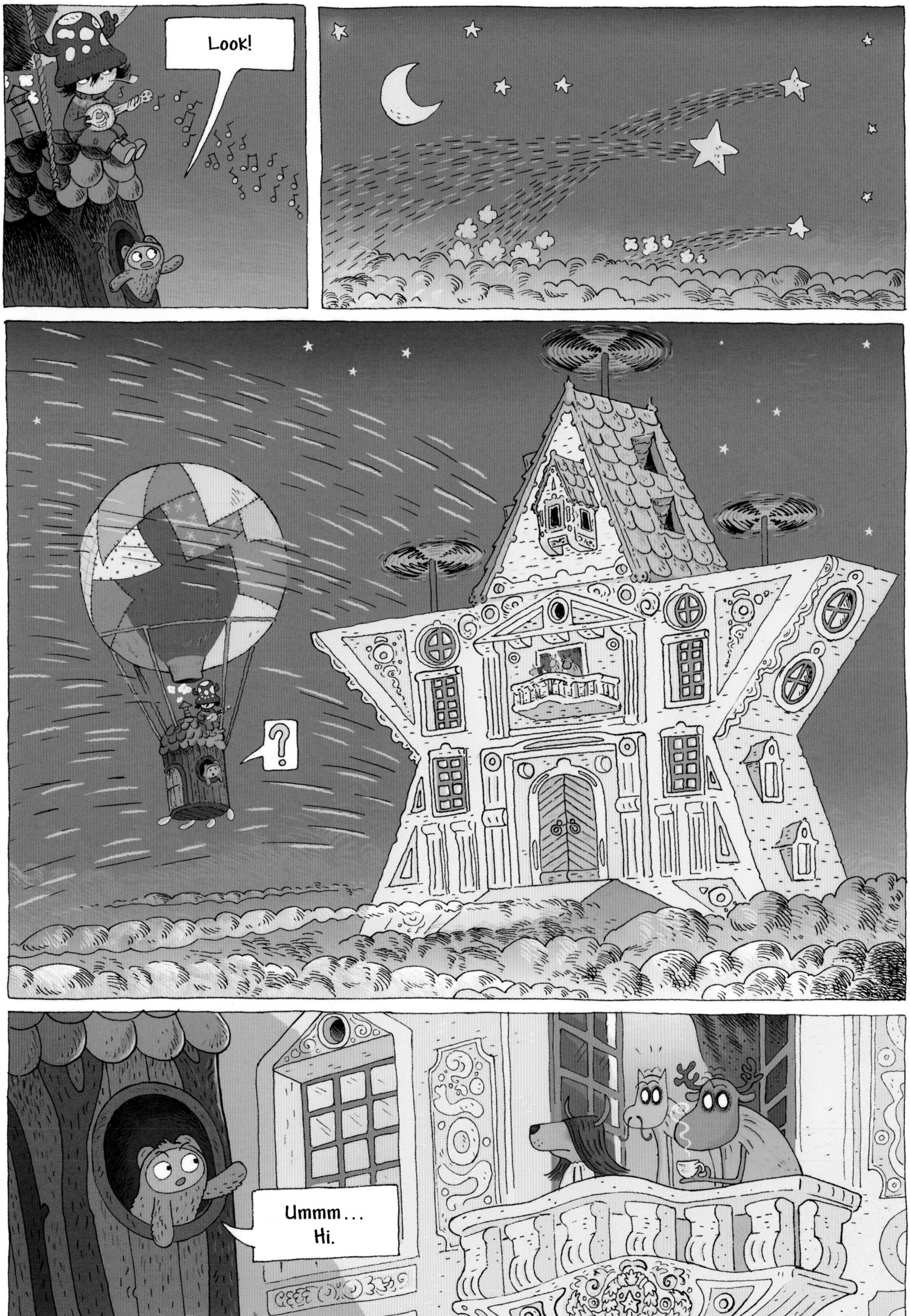
Look!
?
Ummm... Hi.

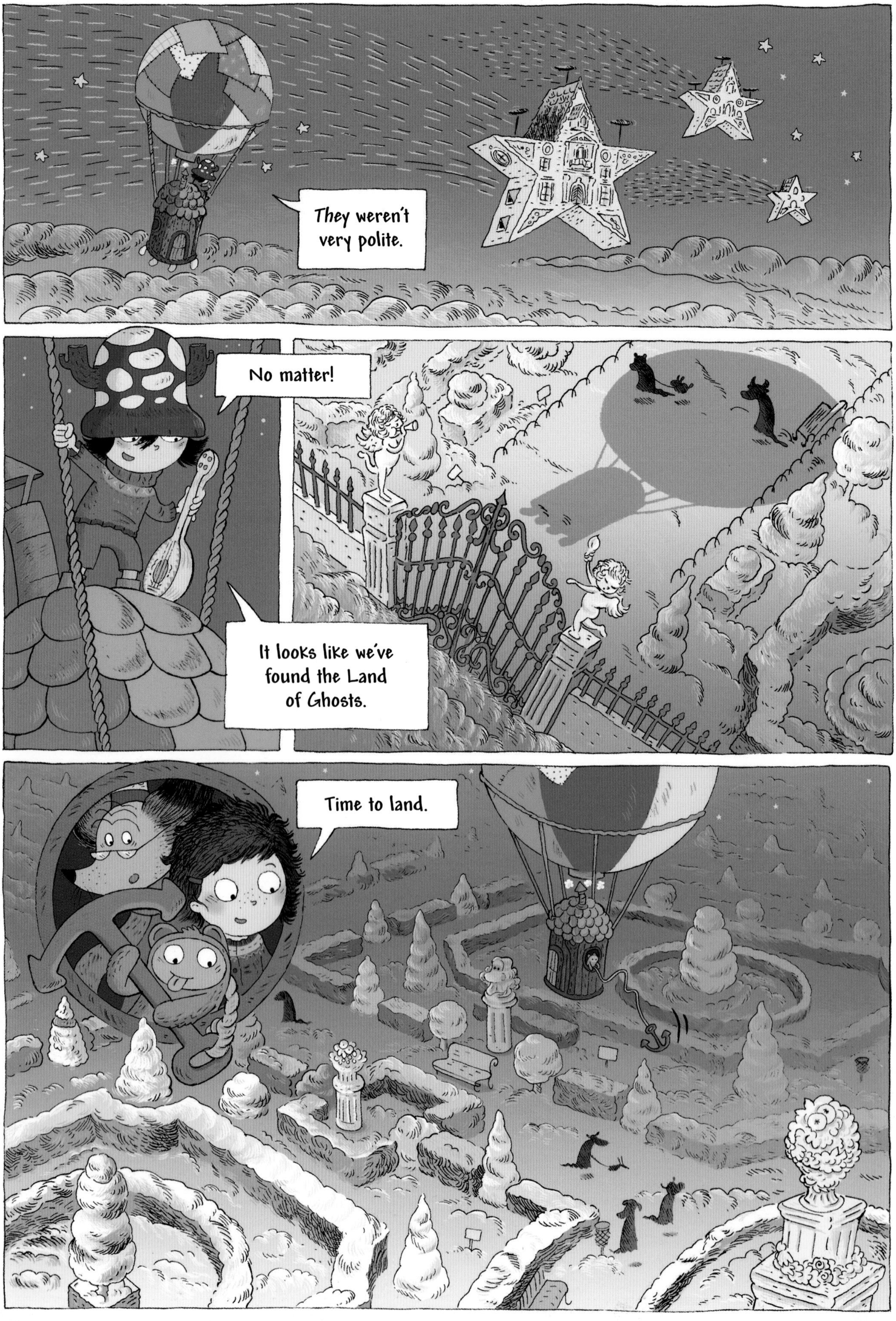
They weren't very polite.
No matter!
It looks like we've found the Land of Ghosts.
Time to land.

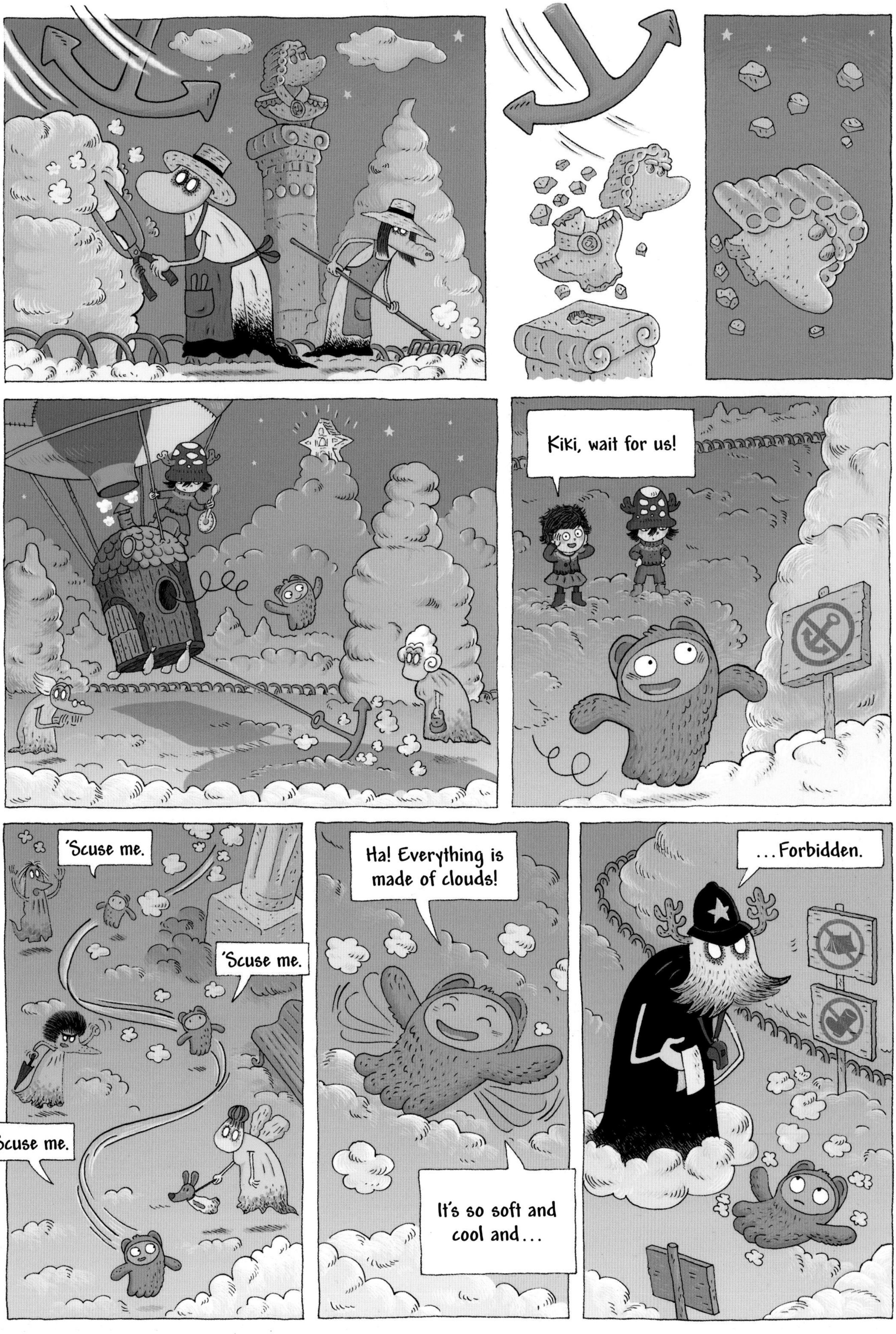
Kiki, wait for us!
'Scuse me.
'Scuse me.
'Scuse me.
Ha! Everything is made of clouds!
It's so soft and cool and...
...Forbidden.

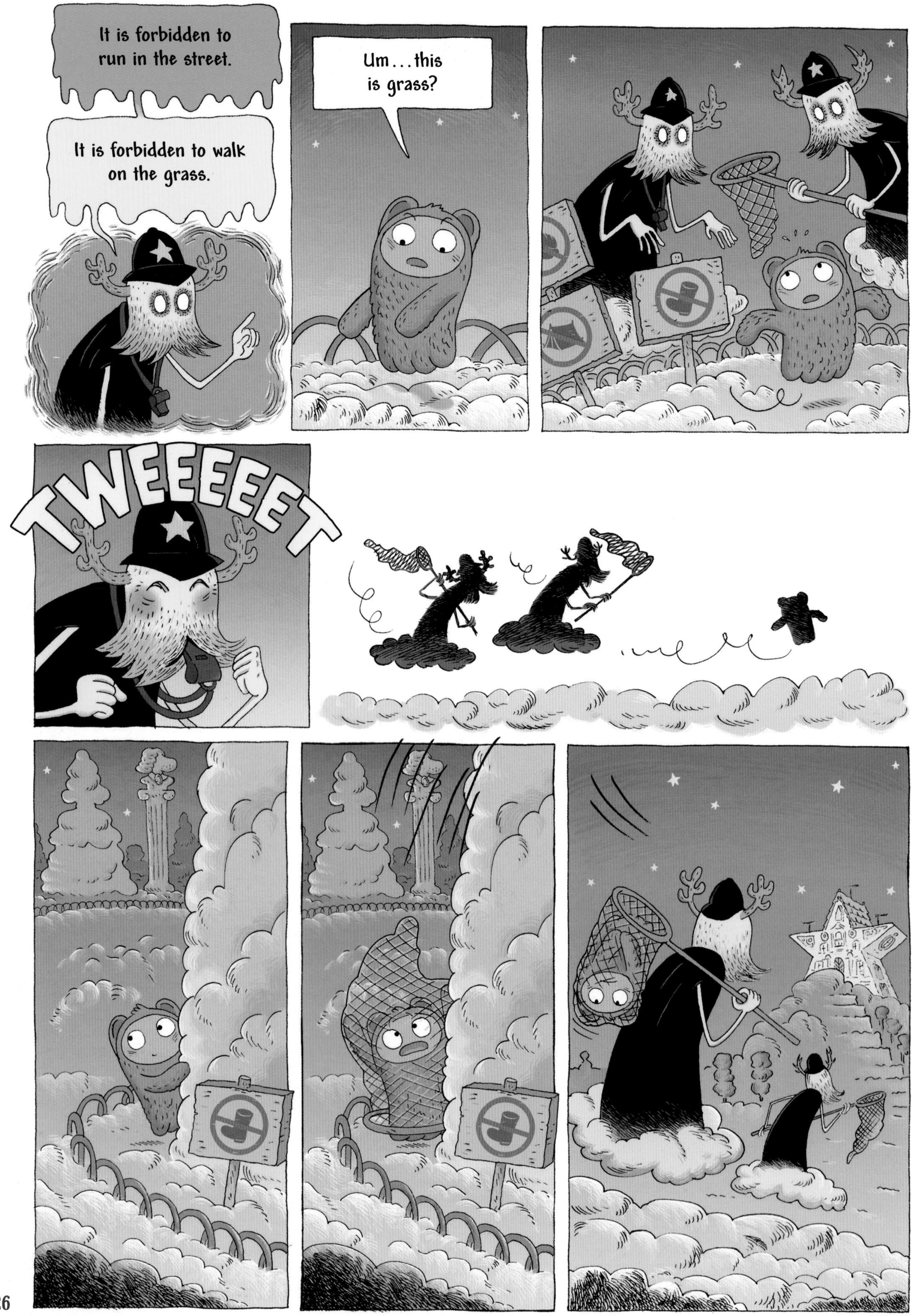
It is forbidden to run in the street.
It is forbidden to walk on the grass.
Um...this is grass?
TWEEEEET

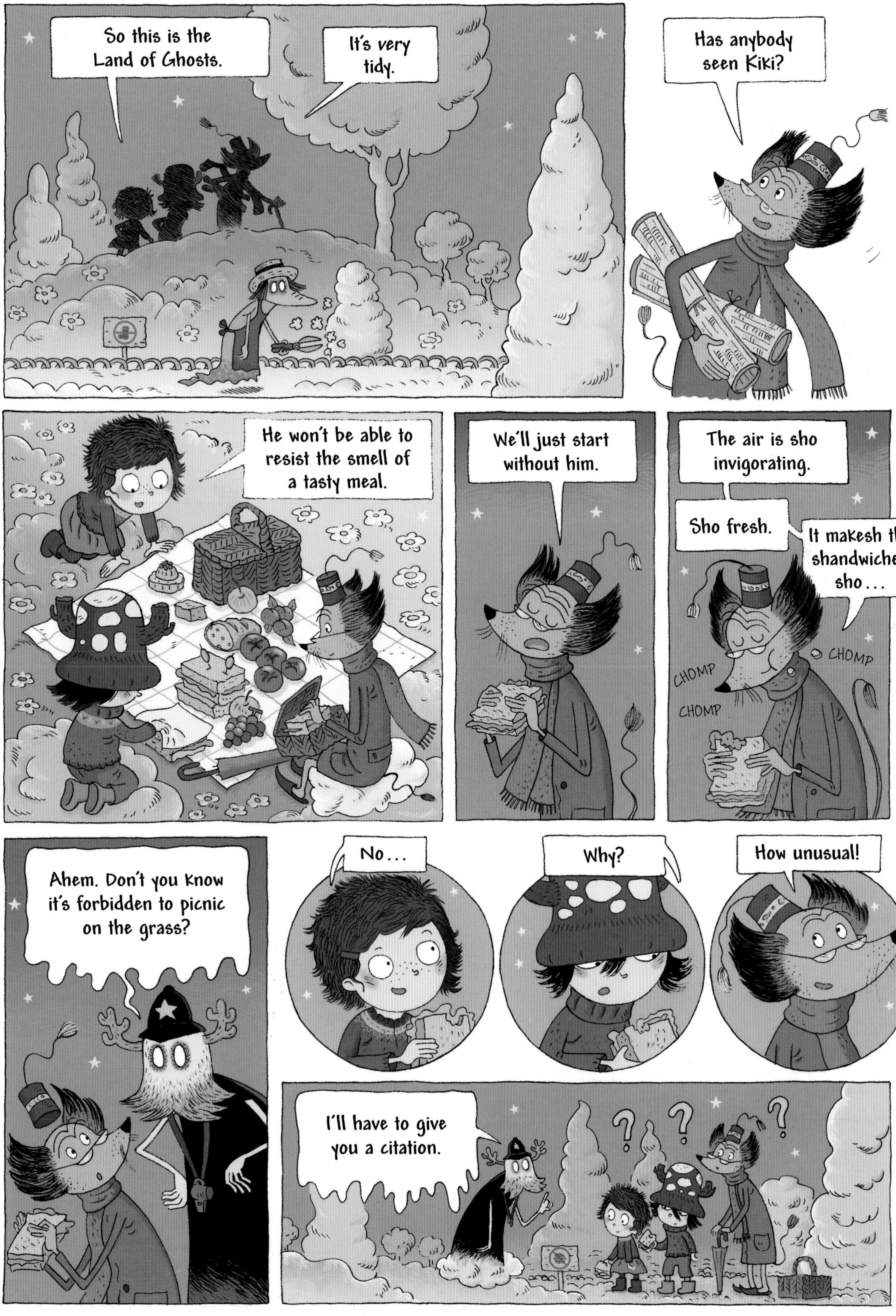
So this is the Land of Ghosts.
It's very tidy.
Has anybody seen Kiki?
He won't be able to resist the smell of a tasty meal.
We'll just start without him.
The air is sho invigorating.
Sho fresh.
It makesh the shandwiches sho...
CHOMP
CHOMP
CHOMP
Ahem. Don't you know it's forbidden to picnic on the grass?
No...
Why?
How unusual!
I'll have to give you a citation.
?
?
?

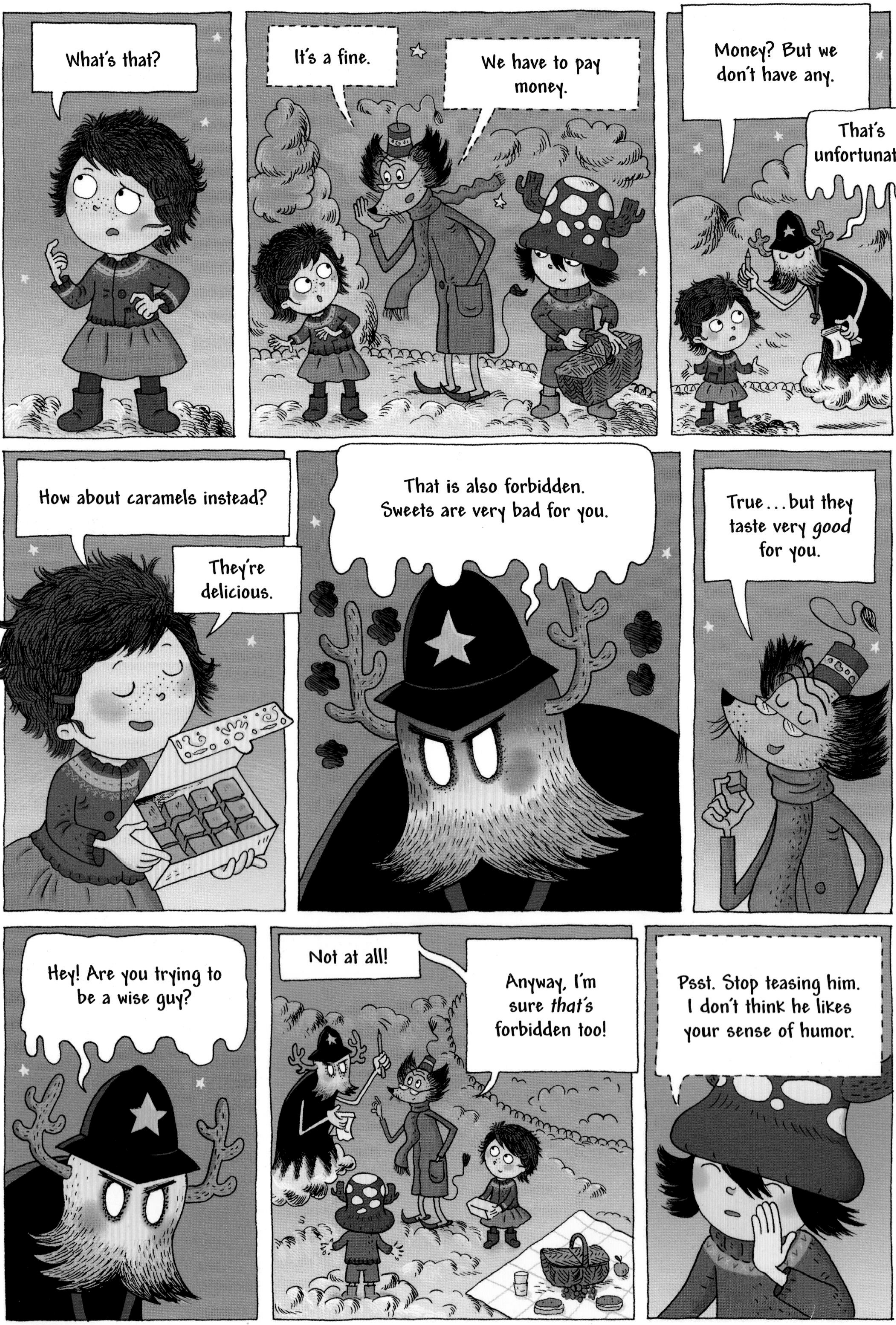

What's that?
It's a fine.
We have to pay money.
Money? But we don't have any.
That's unfortunate.
How about caramels instead?
They're delicious.
That is also forbidden. Sweets are very bad for you.
True...but they taste very *good* for you.
Hey! Are you trying to be a wise guy?
Not at all!
Anyway, I'm sure *that's* forbidden too!
Psst. Stop teasing him. I don't think he likes your sense of humor.

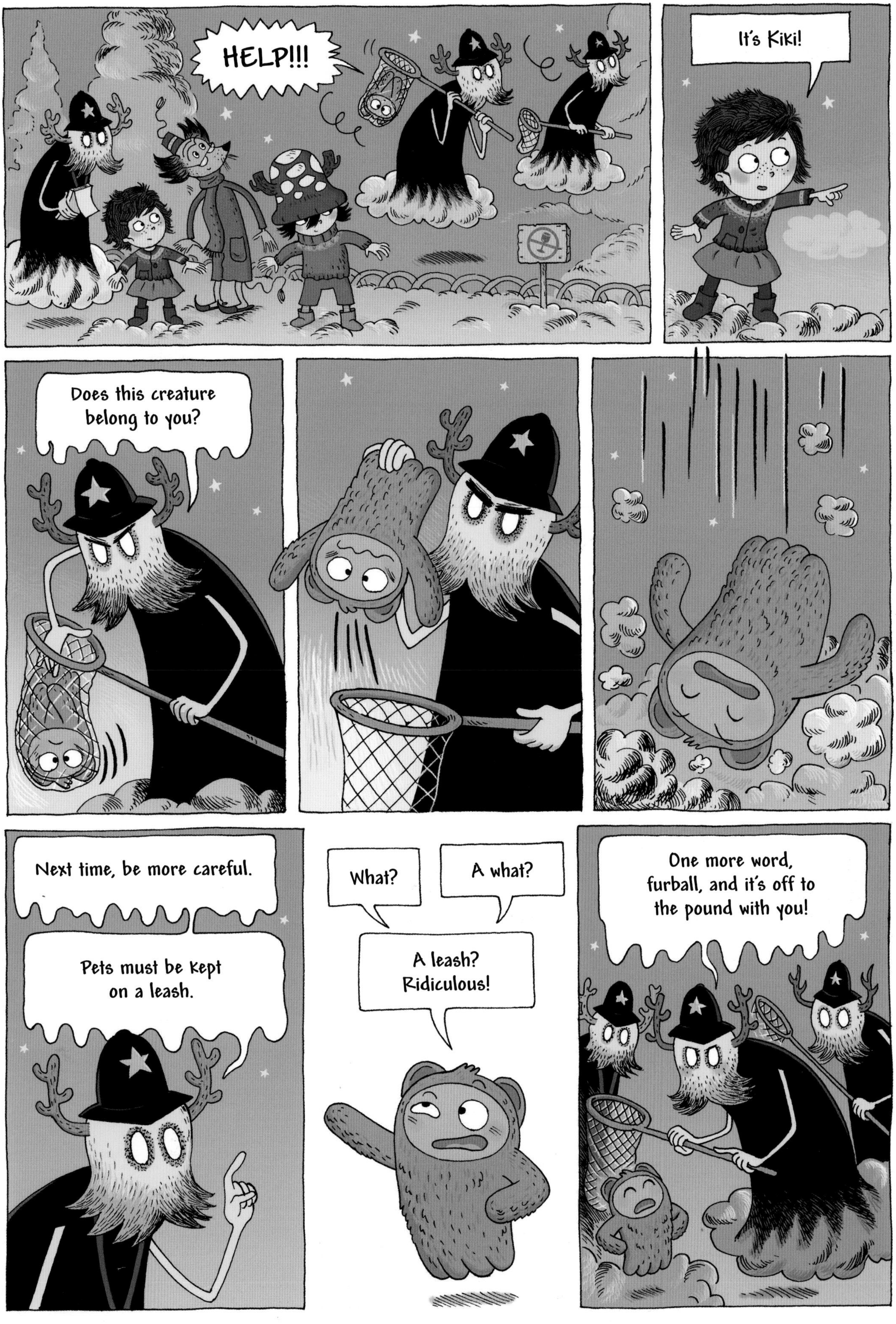
HELP!!!
It's Kiki!
Does this creature belong to you?
Next time, be more careful.
Pets must be kept on a leash.
What?
A what?
A leash? Ridiculous!
One more word, furball, and it's off to the pound with you!

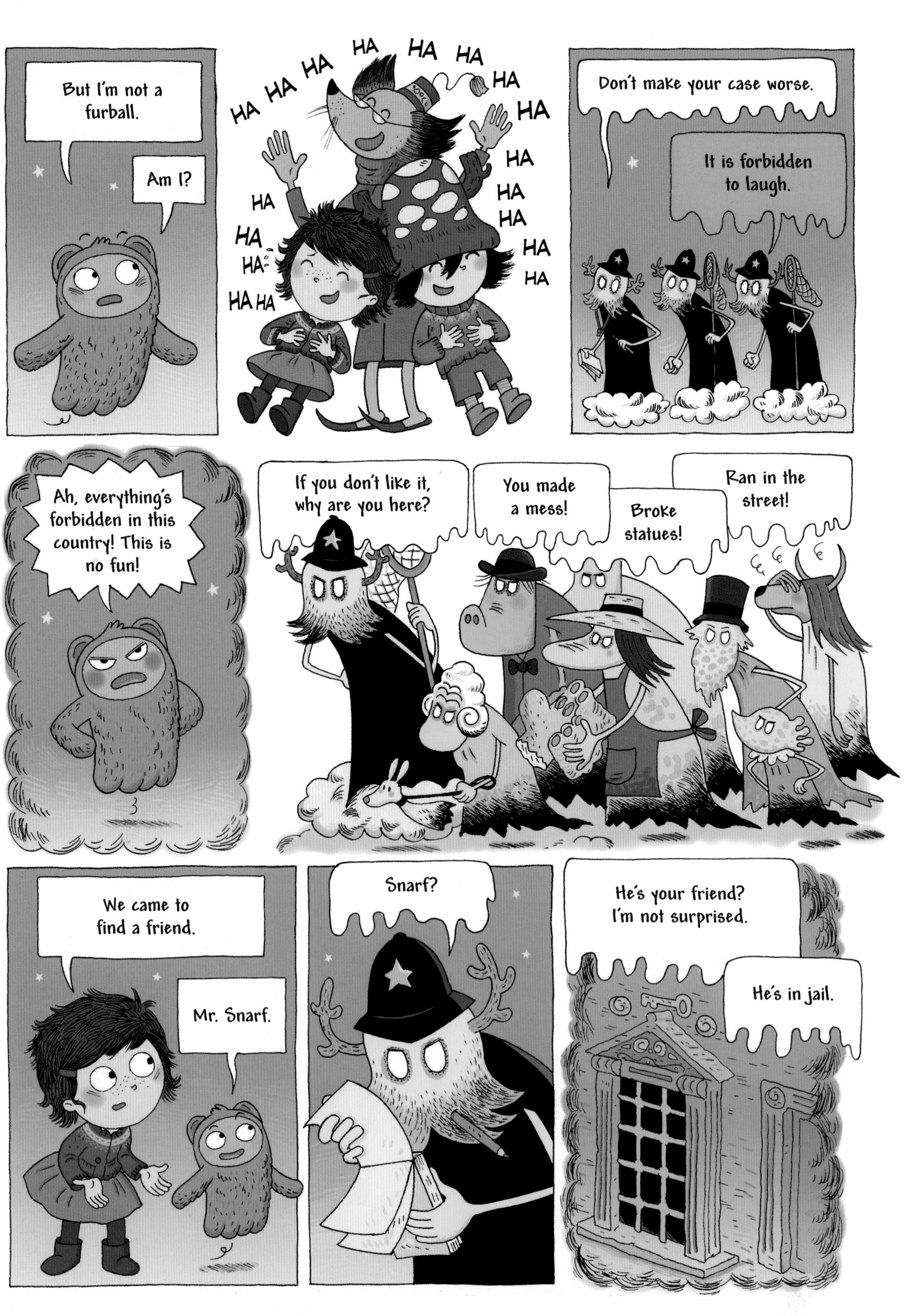
But I'm not a furball.
Am I?
HA HA HA HA HA HA HA HA HA HA HA HA HA HA HA HA HA HA HA
Don't make your case worse.
It is forbidden to laugh.
Ah, everything's forbidden in this country! This is no fun!
If you don't like it, why are you here?
You made a mess!
Broke statues!
Ran in the street!
We came to find a friend.
Mr. Snarf.
Snarf?
He's your friend? I'm not surprised.
He's in jail.

IN JAIL?

But why?

On top of breaking the rules...

...he sneezed.

Many times!

And what?

That's forbidden?

...BRLL BLL R BBB BLLL BRLB LLL BRLLL BLL...

OOOOOOOOOOOHH!!

Making faces at an officer! To jail! At once!

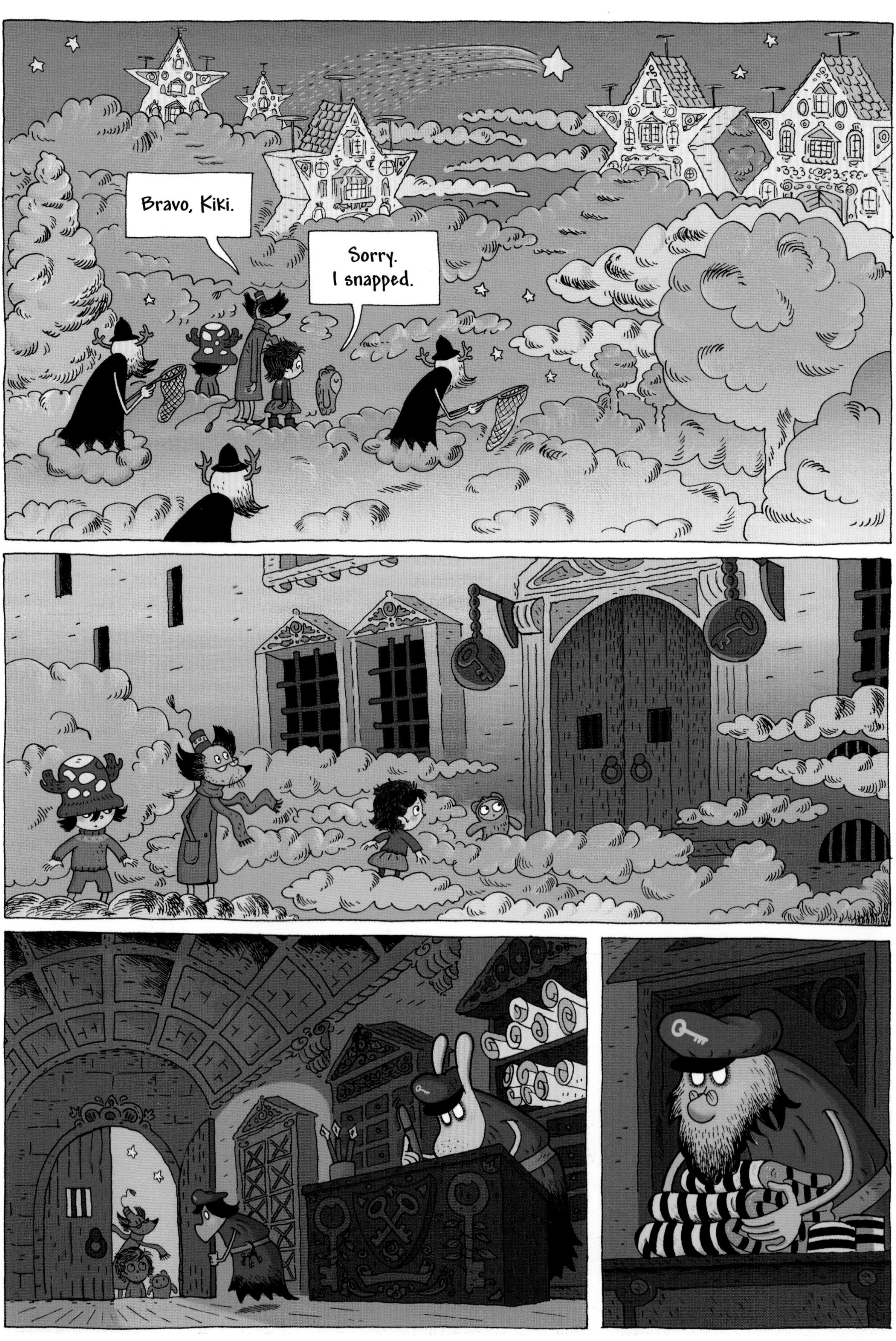
Bravo, Kiki.
Sorry. I snapped.

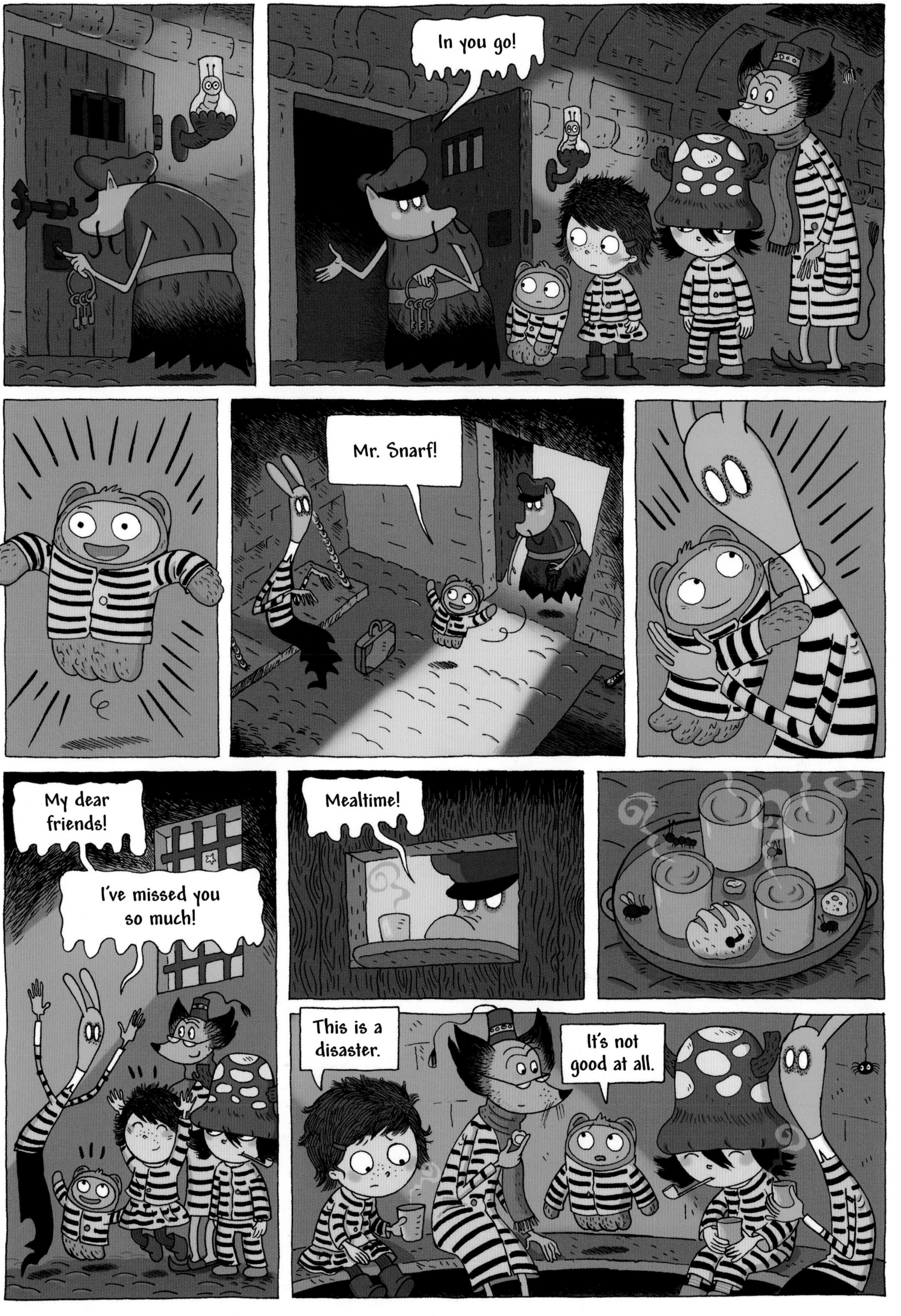
In you go!
Mr. Snarf!
My dear friends!
I've missed you so much!
Mealtime!
This is a disaster.
It's not good at all.

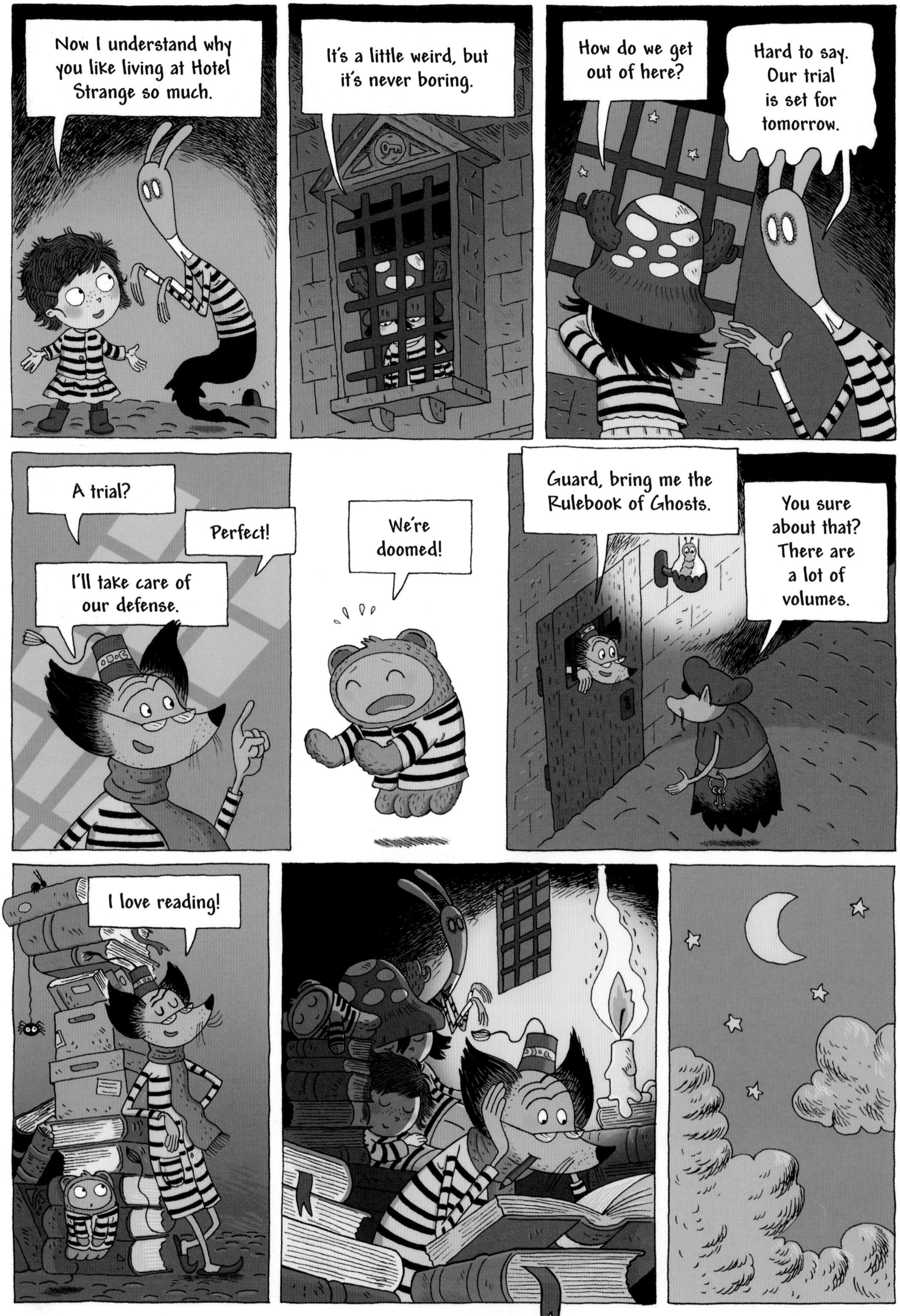
Now I understand why you like living at Hotel Strange so much.
It's a little weird, but it's never boring.
How do we get out of here?
Hard to say. Our trial is set for tomorrow.
A trial?
Perfect!
I'll take care of our defense.
We're doomed!
Guard, bring me the Rulebook of Ghosts.
You sure about that? There are a lot of volumes.
I love reading!

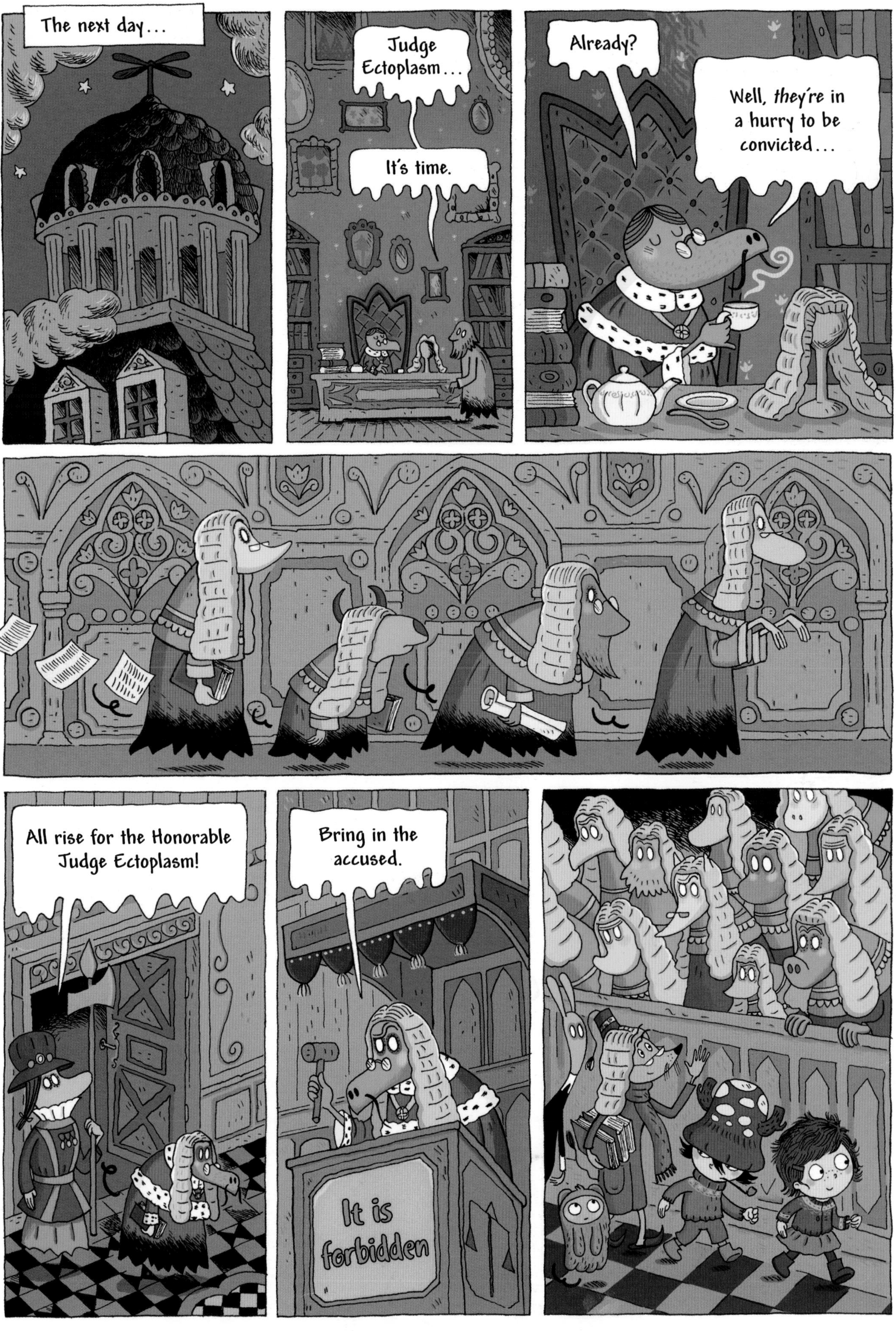
The next day...
Judge Ectoplasm...
It's time.
Already?
Well, *they're* in a hurry to be convicted...
All rise for the Honorable Judge Ectoplasm!
Bring in the accused.
It is forbidden

Clerk, please read the list of crimes.

It is forbidden

blah blah blah blah blah blah blah
blah blah blah blah blah blah blah
blah blah blah blah blah blah blah
blah blah blah blah blah blah
blah blah bla blah blah blah
blah blah lah blah blah
blah blah blah blah
blah blah blah blah
blah bla lah blah
blah bla blah

Very troubling. Verrry troubling.

Do you understand the charges against you?

Yes!

In short: Everything is forbidden...

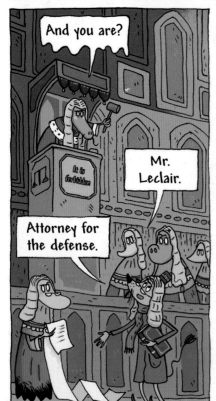
And you are?

It is forbidden

Mr. Leclair.

Attorney for the defense.

You're very bold.

whisper   whisper   whisper

whisper

Your Honor, I demand our immediate freedom. And also freedom for our friend Mr. Snarf.

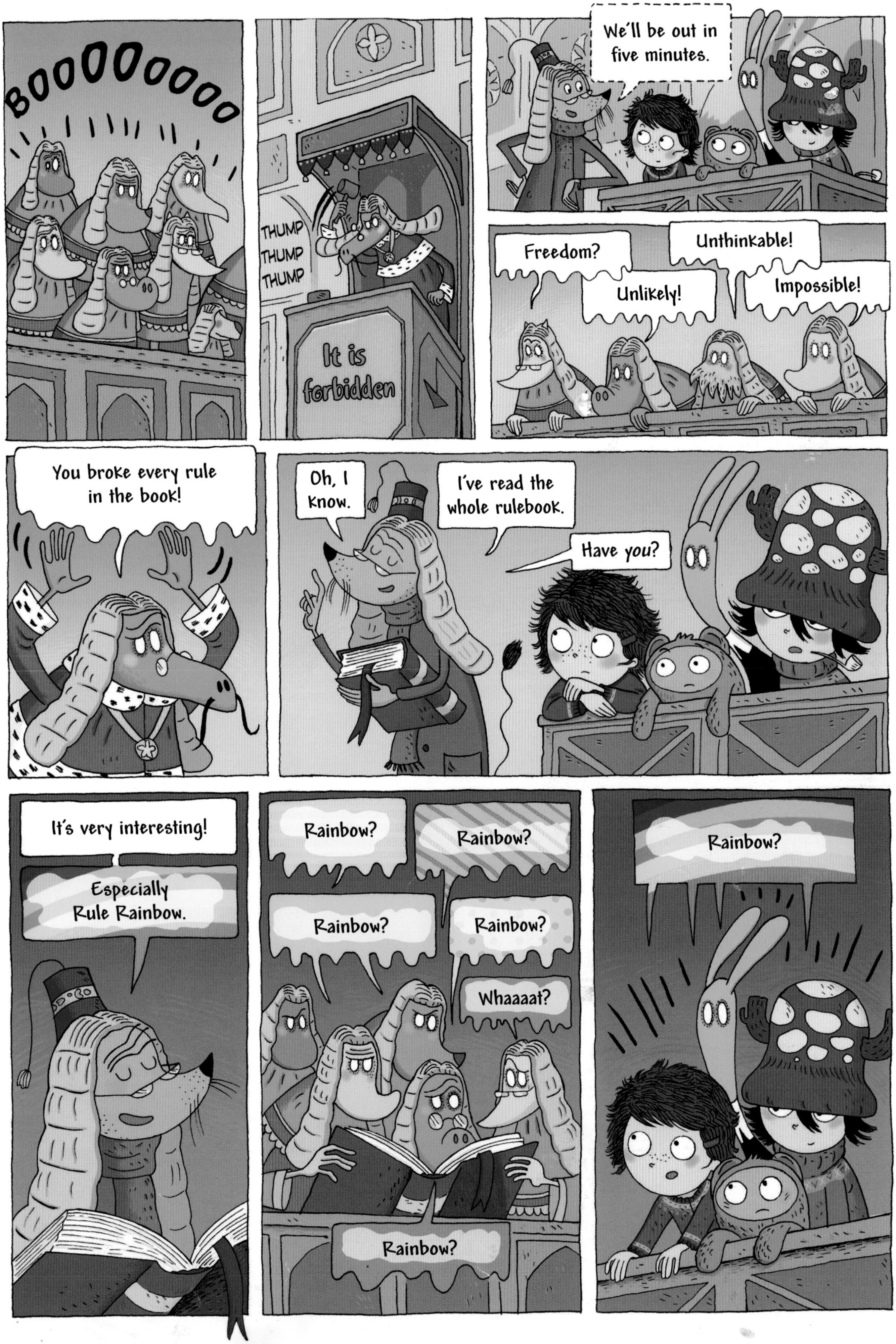
BOOOOoooo
THUMP
THUMP
THUMP
It is forbidden
We'll be out in five minutes.
Freedom?
Unthinkable!
Unlikely!
Impossible!
You broke every rule in the book!
Oh, I know.
I've read the whole rulebook.
Have you?
It's very interesting!
Especially Rule Rainbow.
Rainbow?
Rainbow?
Rainbow?
Rainbow?
Whaaaat?
Rainbow?
Rainbow?

Show me that.

mumble mumble rumble rumble grumble...

Rule Rainbow: It is forbidden to forbid!

Why haven't I seen this rule!?

Two pages were stuck together, Your Honor.

In that case...you're free to go.

Yippee! We're going home!

Splendid, Mr. Leclair!

Bravo!

Congratulations!

How clever!

Really, pure genius!

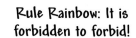

38

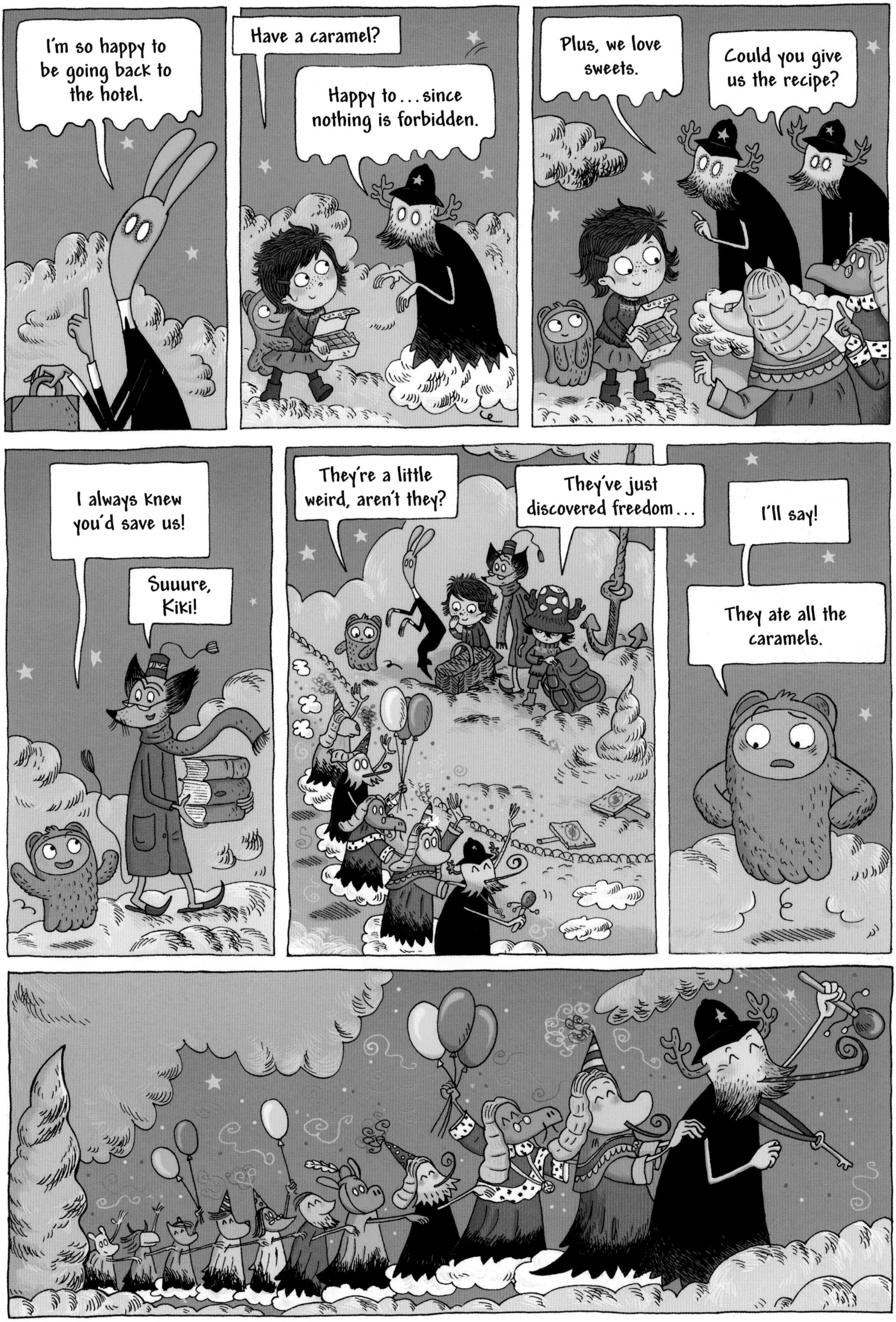
I'm so happy to be going back to the hotel.
Have a caramel?
Happy to... since nothing is forbidden.
Plus, we love sweets.
Could you give us the recipe?
I always knew you'd save us!
Suuure, Kiki!
They're a little weird, aren't they?
They've just discovered freedom...
I'll say!
They ate all the caramels.

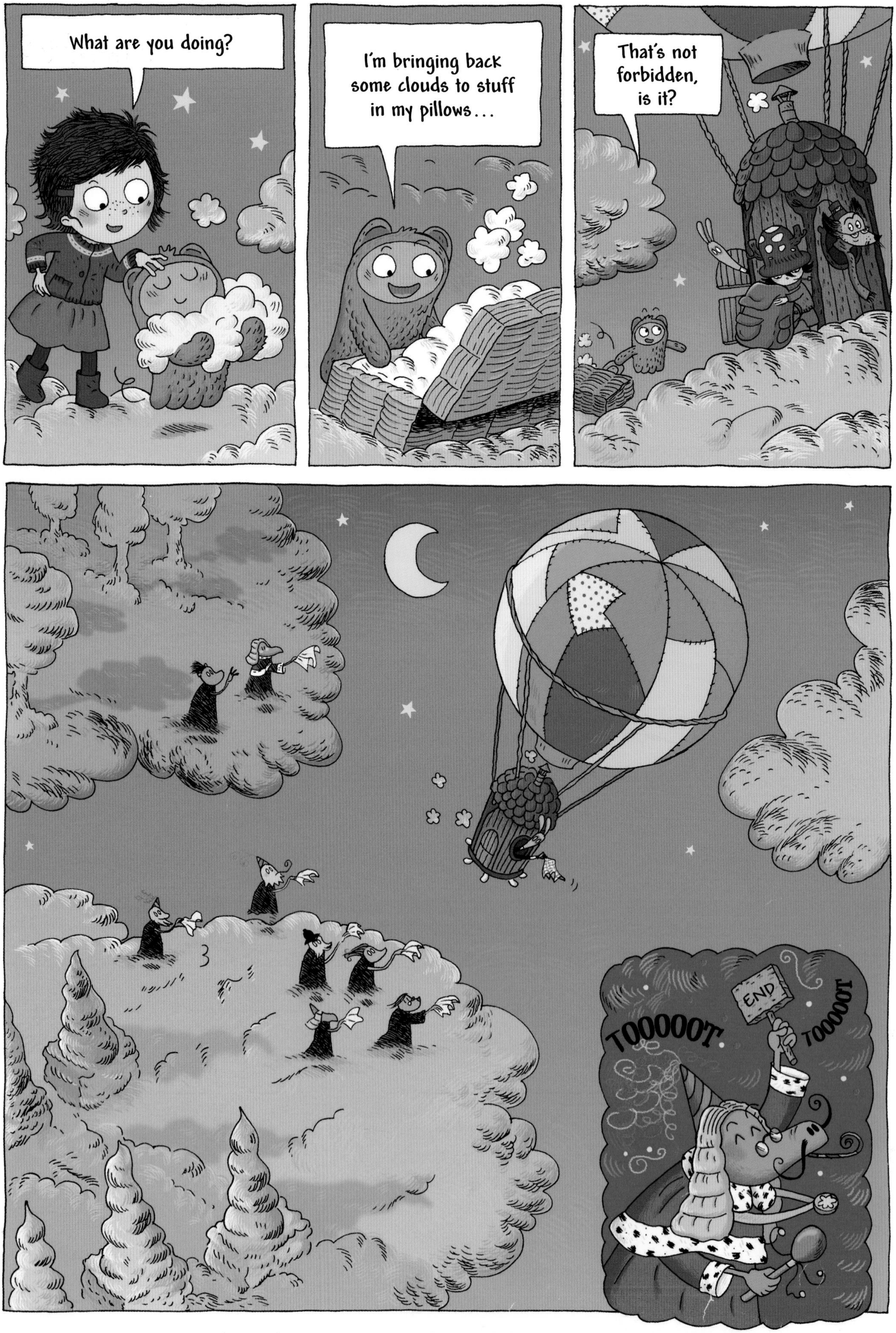
What are you doing?
I'm bringing back some clouds to stuff in my pillows...
That's not forbidden, is it?
END
TOOOOOT
TOOOOOT

Caramels

Ask an adult for help in the kitchen.

2 plus 6 tablespoons butter
⅔ cup granulated sugar
1 tablespoon honey
14 ounces sweetened condensed milk

1. Cut out a 12-inch by 12-inch sheet of parchment paper, and line a baking pan. To avoid caramels that stick to the sheet, spread 2 tablespoons of butter on the parchment paper.
2. In a small saucepan, mix 6 tablespoons of butter with sugar, honey, and condensed milk.
3. Heat the saucepan on a low temperature. Stir the mixture for about 20 minutes, until it has a nice light brown color.
4. Pour the mixture into the baking pan.
5. Spread out the mixture with a spatula into a 8-inch by 8-inch square.
6. Let the mixture cool, and then cut it into small candy-size squares.

And ta-da! Your caramels are ready!

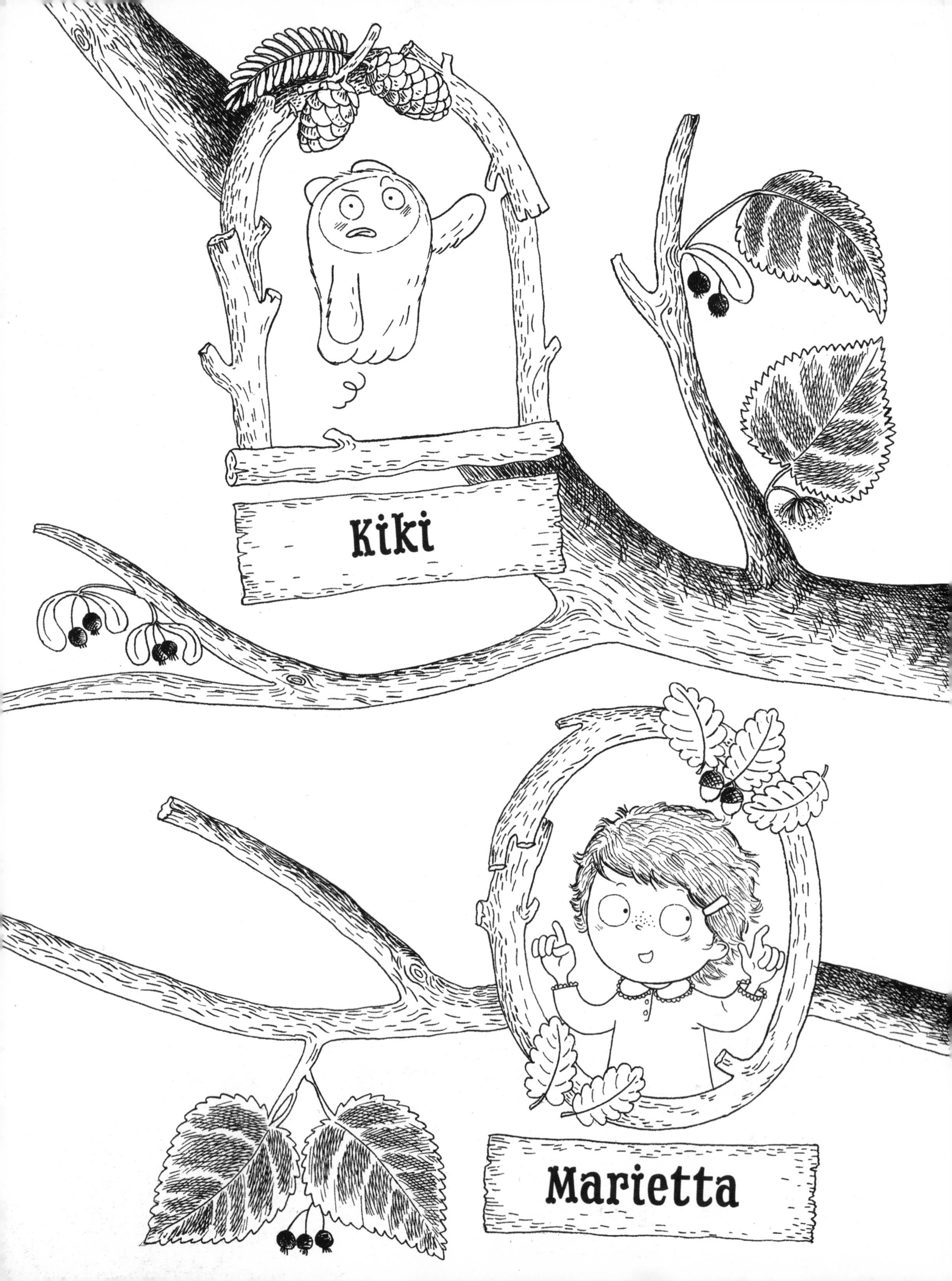
Kiki
Marietta

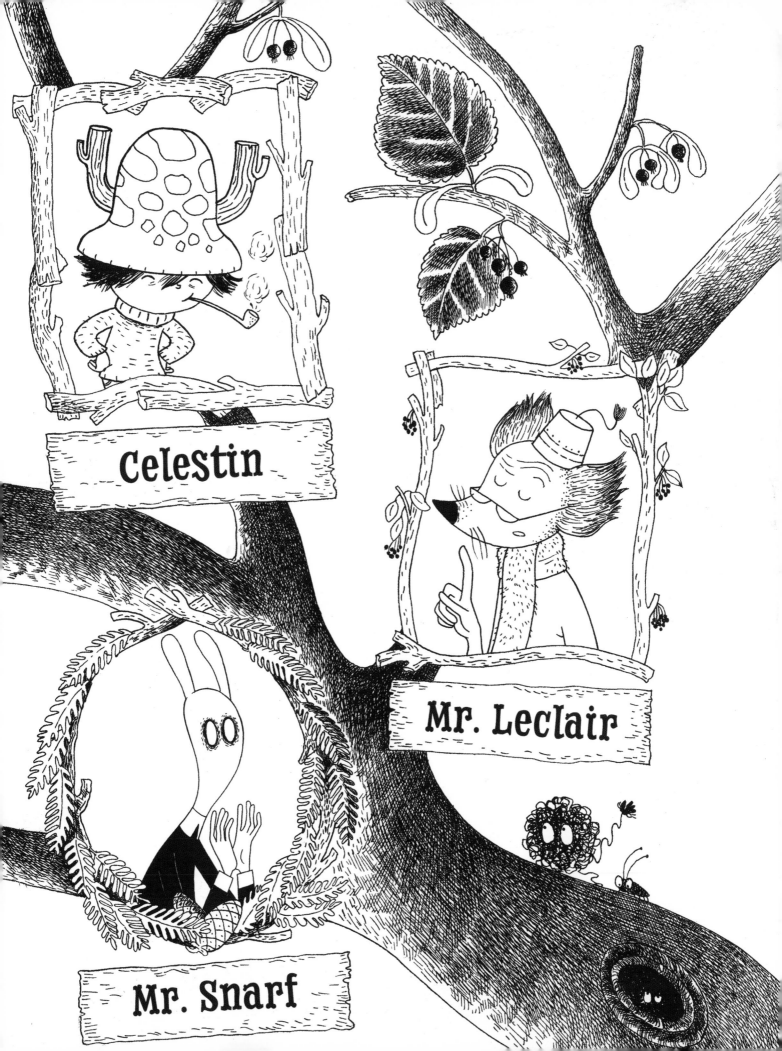

Celestin

Mr. Leclair

Mr. Snarf